GATHER THE ANARCHISTS

TILLY WALLACE

To be the first to hear about Tilly's new releases and exclusive offers, sign up at:

https://www.tillywallace.com/newsletter

Chapter One

THURSDAY, *15 April, 1920*

My heart pounded so rapidly in my chest that I worried it might explode and ruin the delicate aqua silk in my hands. I closed my eyes and drew a breath.

Everything will be fine, I reassured myself.

Every minute of the evening had been planned and gone over for potential flaws more times than any military campaign. Nothing would go wrong. Mrs Cooper, my formidable mentor and general of the event, would never allow it. If Mrs Cooper had been put in charge of the Gallipoli landing, our troops might have fared better.

"It's perfect, Mrs Devine. You can leave it alone now," Etty's voice came from my side.

"Are you sure?" I got off my knees and narrowed my gaze at the ensemble. I thought it was perfect, but would our guests? Did I need to move the sash just a fraction more to the left? Or perhaps we should have chosen a different shoe in a darker hue of navy.

"I'm sure. Let her go and wait with the others." Etty waved the model to the door. The promotion to my second in command, or workroom manager, had brought out a new confidence in Etty. She fussed over the models like a broody hen and had no problems with giving me a peck to move along!

The evening of my little showing to celebrate the opening of the new space had finally arrived. After hiring two more seamstresses full-time, and enlisting Mrs Mac, who usually designed the costumes at the Cricket, the five of us had managed to produce twelve complete outfits to unveil to a select audience. The gowns were intended to delight my clients and, I hoped, give flight to their imaginations as to what we could create together. I also hoped the wealthy women would gossip like fishwives and spread the word that Grace Designs was a force to be reckoned with in the world of fashion in New Zealand.

We had laboured for two full days to transform the workroom. The cutting table had been pushed to one side of the room and it now held drinks and nibbles and a gorgeous central display of flowers. Mrs Cooper's staff circulated among the guests, carrying silver trays holding champagne and teeny mouthfuls of food. Curvaceous chairs with plush velvet padded seats were arrayed in a semi-circle. We used the new fitting rooms to get the models ready, then they would walk into the workroom and parade in front of the guests before returning to change outfits.

We had four girls of similar build, all drawn from Etty's friend circle. Mrs Cooper had drilled them in how to walk and turn, and they now glided across the floor like French models. Each model had a dedicated fitting room with her three outfits for the evening, and Etty and I would swoop as soon as the girl had finished her circuit of the room.

Sam stood in the lobby, leaning on the curved reception desk. Dressed in a navy suit that bordered on black and with a silver watch chain draped from waistcoat buttonhole to pocket, she was the image of suave elegance. "Ready to start? That lot have finished their first drinks and are onto their second."

I drew a deep breath. The time had come to affix the bayonet to my rifle and go over the top, as our lads did during the war. If they could charge across the battlefield in the face of hostile fire, I could face thirty sets of critical eyes on the home ground of my atelier.

I nodded. "Ready."

Sam took hold of my hand and squeezed. "It's going to be an incredible night. I am so proud of you."

Love for my friend overrode the panic building inside me. "I couldn't have done it without you. Or without everyone who has supported me." From Mrs Cooper with her unwavering belief and not-so-gentle prodding along, to Dad, who turned the old boarding house into an atelier. Sam, who always had my back.

Etty, the most amazing assistant who now blossomed as my right-hand woman.

The four models lined up, ready to sashay into the workroom. We had hired a quartet of musicians who sat beside the cutting table and played soft jazz music. The lullaby drifted through the building and soothed my nerves as I hummed along to the tune.

The door at the end of the hall cracked open and Harry appeared, wearing a tweed suit offset with a deep cerise tie and a matching pocket square. He had healed from the horrible beating he sustained in a dark alley, and the experience made us closer friends. He looked dapper and a tad nervous, clutching a wad of cardboard cards. When the librarian heard about the planned fashion showing, he volunteered to narrate the evening. I had written out details of each outfit for him that he would read as the girl displayed the clothing.

"Shall we begin?" he asked.

I nodded, too nervous to talk. Sam thrust a glass of champagne at me, and I took a quick sip. But not too much. It wouldn't pay to get drunk when I might need to fix a hem quickly or offer intelligent conversation to a potential client.

Harry kissed my cheek and walked back to the open door.

"Ladies," he called their attention to him. "You are in for a *divine* treat this evening. We start with this bold daywear look in vertical navy blue and white stripes. The business-like collar is alleviated by the playful lace around the edge."

The first model walked into the room. Harry's voice carried over the gasps and murmurs. I couldn't look. We had to ensure as soon as the model finished, we were ready to hustle her into the fitting room, peel the clothes off her back, and dress her in the next outfit.

The daywear looks all incorporated outerwear with a selection of coats and capes. Harry kept up his steady commentary as the display moved into the late afternoon and then evening wear—both informal and formal. These delicious creations were what the guests had really come to see. I thought we had outdone ourselves, pushing to the very edge of fashion. One gown revealed knees. *Knees!* I hoped no one would faint at the sight.

The evening passed in a blur of fabrics. When one girl finished her slow circuit, she came back to a fitting room where Etty and I pounced like tigers waiting in long grass. I couldn't stop myself tweaking the hang of chiffon here, or the placement of a drape there. Etty had to almost haul me backwards and gesture for her friend to go.

Soon, it was time for the ultimate piece. My flight of fancy and one of pure extravagance—the fantail evening gown. The tail feathers spread out behind the model like a peacock's tail dragging on the ground, but a cunning arrangement underneath allowed them to be swept up when dancing and held to one side. We had spent hours embroidering each fabric feather with metallic thread to create the effect of the rachis down the middle and the vane. We used muted colours like the little bird, but they still conveyed warmth and richness. Feathers in a rich bronze covered the bodice, and they ruffled gently up to the collarbone. The model looked like a fantail turned human by magic.

"Oh," I whispered when I stood back. Unable to say more, I held my hands to my face. For me, this gown was a true labour of love. The inspiration was the chatty little bird who flitted past me as I walked in the Botanic Garden. How I wished I was the one wearing it. What a dream it would be to dance the night away with a handsome partner while wearing my special evening dress.

"She's beautiful," Etty said as her friend straightened her back and took slow and measured steps through the doorway.

I couldn't look as she made her way into the workroom. What if they didn't like it?

Gasps rippled back along the hall. Then came the applause. Pure joy flooded through every part of me, and I threw my arms around Etty.

"We did it," I said.

Harry shot out into the hall and held out his hand to me. "Come on, your turn now."

Oh...no. I didn't enjoy being the centre of attention. Before I could decline his request, Sam grabbed hold of my other hand and the two of them hauled me towards the door. It seems I would face my clients and guests after all.

"Ladies, may I present the extremely talented woman behind tonight's showing...Mrs Grace Devine,"

Harry said. Then, with a sweep of his arm, he stood to one side to reveal me. Sam let go and gave me a friendly nudge to propel me into the room.

The guests clapped, and some called out *bravo*. Mrs Cooper beamed like a Cheshire cat. Not knowing what to do, I dropped a curtsey. Tears misted my eyes. I couldn't remember being this overwhelmed and happy since the midwife laid a newborn Theo in my arms.

Mrs Cooper's staff circulated with trays of macaroons and other sweet treats as the guests rose for a closer look at the designs. The models held poses. My staff wheeled the other gowns in on their headless forms and positioned them around the room.

"Well done, my girl." Mrs Cooper took my hand and kissed my cheek. "You are a triumph. They shall talk of nothing else this week."

"I couldn't have done it without you, Mrs Cooper. You did a marvellous job on the models, and I am ever so grateful for your staff working this evening." I gestured to the two maids carrying trays.

"I consider it an investment. I rather fancy the idea of eventually letting this entire building to you, but you need to grow large enough to afford the rent." She grinned and toasted me with her glass.

The cunning woman. All those years mentoring and encouraging me just to ensure she had a tenant for one of her properties! How many seamstresses would I need beavering away to occupy the entire building? I laughed at the idea, certain that she had joked with me. Hadn't she?

"Now, go and take new commissions from these ladies while they are all giddy from champagne and your glorious designs." Mrs Cooper nudged me in the direction of a group of four well-heeled ladies.

One lady, a slender blonde, was Miss Fleur Belmont. A shining light on the Wellington social scene. She was a dream to dress. Although her taste was more conservative than Mrs Taylor, one of my favourite clients, who chatted loudly in another corner. The other three women were potential clients, invited to the evening by Mrs Cooper, and they all appeared acquaintances of Miss Belmont.

"I hope you enjoyed the evening, ladies," I murmured as I approached.

"Fabulous, Mrs Devine. I have my eye on the striped daywear, in my signature colours, of course," Miss Belmont said.

Her signature colours were a range of dreamy pinks through to lush fuchsia. "I think I have just the fabric. Would you care to make an appointment with Miss Doyle to discuss the details?"

I indicated Etty, who carried the appointment book ready to round up as many keen customers as we could handle.

"Absolutely, Mrs D. My friend Violet is frightfully keen on a dress or two, as well." Using the hand clutching a glass of champagne, Miss Belmont tapped her knuckles against the arm of the woman beside her.

"Which gowns caught your eye, Miss Steadman?" I had memorised names and Mrs Cooper's descriptions of the potential new clients, so I could address them directly. Miss Steadman had a similar pale colouring to Miss Belmont but lacked the few extra inches of height her friend possessed.

"I rather liked the skirt and blouse combinations, and there was an evening dress with lemon beading that was stunning," she said, with a bright sparkle in her eyes.

The third of Miss Belmont's friends was a curvy brunette with a dour look, as though she found the entire evening boring and not to her taste. From what Mrs Cooper had told me, she was a Russian emigree, and her family were fabulously rich. Wealthy or not, I refused to let one grumpy person diminish my excitement for the evening and concentrated on those who wanted to discuss fabrics, embellishments and possible alterations. My mind swam with a kaleidoscope of colours and combinations, and I was sure that tomorrow would bring a terrible headache from the overindulgence of all the wonderful things. Rather like when Theo ate a whole stick of candy floss.

Etty scribbled notes in the appointment book and had a feverish grin whenever I caught her eye. I could burst. Everything had turned out so marvellous.

The evening neared its end as I approached Mrs Taylor, who stood by the window staring at the lane below. She beamed as I neared. "Brilliant showing, Mrs Devine. An absolutely lovely collection. But perhaps a little too conservative for my taste."

I laughed. "You are a rarity, Mrs Taylor. Your

clothing is at least two seasons ahead of the trend. Most women are nervous forging the path and much prefer to follow." I adored designing for the close friend of Mrs Cooper. While not a conventional shape and over fifty, she had a zest for life that embodied every piece of fabric draped on her form.

"Do say you have something special tucked away for me?" She winked.

"I may have a bold, geometric print in burnt orange and rust that will make a stunning autumn day outfit." I often bought fabrics with clients in mind, then crossed my fingers that they fell in love with them. While we were late to consider autumn clothing when that season was already upon us, Mrs Taylor could wear such an outfit on any chilly day.

"I already have an appointment for next week. We shall discuss it then." She patted my arm.

The guests took their leave, and Mrs Cooper's maids tidied away the glasses, plates, and trays. We packed everything into boxes to load into Mrs Cooper's travelling vehicle for the trip back to her home.

In the fitting room, I helped the last model from her gown.

"Thank you for your hard work this evening," I said as I undid the row of shell buttons. "We might not be in London, but I think we can hold our own here in New Zealand."

"I think we are better, Mrs Devine. You work hard here, and you can get ahead. Over there, the aristocracy keeps everyone down." Bridget held her hair out of the way as I found the last button at her nape.

Mrs Cooper often regaled me with tales of her life in England as a minor noble. It all sounded horribly complicated with who had to curtsey to whom, or who could walk into dinner first. The pecking order was set in stone, but at least with chickens, you could rise in the ranks.

As I helped Bridget out of her dress, my hand grazed her shoulder. In the excitement of the evening, I had grown careless about touching exposed skin. The memory leapt from her torso and burrowed into my mind.

A man with shining eyes took my hand. "You wait and see. We'll show the world. Never again will England keep honest men down and stomp on our heads. We will break free of her chains."

The vitriol in the man's voice was a dose of cold water on my mood. Luckily, my silence was easy to mask as I placed the dress back over the naked form in the corner and the model stepped into her own clothes.

<h1 style="text-align:center">Chapter Two</h1>

Friday, the next day, was a subdued one in our workspace. The excitement of the previous night had left a weary silence in its wake. I decided to take advantage of the rare lull and popped out for some fresh air and to run some errands. First, I visited the Kostas Bakery and purchased a well-deserved afternoon tea for my employees. Then I set out to find someone in particular.

A man in his early thirties and of a slight build stood on the corner. Stubble clung to his jawline. Hatless, he instead had a beaten tin crown pressed onto his unruly light brown locks. "I am your true prince! Celebrate my arrival in Wellington!" he yelled at the passersby.

A woman skittered out of the way and quickened her step. A group of men jeered as they walked by.

"Hello, George." Unlike the other pedestrians, I approached him and held out the paper bag in my hands. The bag held a sandwich, a biscuit, and an apple.

"Mrs Devine, you are the most loyal of our subjects." He grinned, and it lit his clear blue eyes like a summer sky. He took the bag and peered inside. "One day I shall make you my queen."

George had no permanent home. Instead, George wandered around the North Island on a bay mare called Meg, and he stabled her up by the Shepherds' Arms when he returned to Wellington. He called his nomadic lifestyle *surveying his dominion*. Whenever I heard he was back in town, I regularly packed an extra lunch to give him. "Oh, gosh. Don't go making me a queen, George. I rather like my quiet little existence here. I don't have the fortitude for all those royal events and dealing with politicians."

Many people avoided George and his outrageous proclamations. He was convinced he was the rightful heir to the British throne, the result of an affair between his mother and King George. His irrefutable proof, his name—George King, and a vague resemblance to the monarch and the Hanoverian blue eyes. Apparently, his mother told him she had been a maid at Buckingham Palace, but she was dispatched to New Zealand when she conceived the royal bastard. Who knew if her story was true or not, but her son latched onto it with both hands. Even if there were a single grain of truth in the tale, George still couldn't inherit the crown unless his alleged royal father had married his mother. But that wasn't a subject I felt I could broach.

"The police are trying to lock me up, you know. They don't want me meeting my half-brother. But I am too cunning for them. I have a plan and supporters at my back." He tapped the side of his nose and winked.

His plan probably involved hiding at the wharf, where he usually made himself a cosy nest among the crates. The night watch turned a blind eye, many of them Irish and with no love for the British royal family.

"Well, you take care of yourself, George. You have promised me a dance at your coronation ball." I saw no harm in stepping into his world, especially when it collided with my dreams. If George were ever recognised as the true heir and a grand ball was held in his honour, I would finally have an opportunity to wear my fantail gown.

Waving goodbye, I carried on my way along Lambton Quay and towards the post office. Pedestrians bustled up and down both sides of the road. Horses trotted along pulling carriages or carts, while faster motorcars swerved around them. There seemed more people than usual as the capital made preparations for events in early May. Excitement swirled through the air. The Prince of Wales would arrive next week in Auckland, on board Britain's newest and largest battleship, the HMS *Renown*, and would begin a month-long tour of New Zealand.

Wellington would host not one but *two* balls in his honour. The first at Government House would be attended by the elite of Wellington society and numerous politicians. The second would be held in the Town Hall and was called the Citizens Ball. Invitations were highly sought after. Despite its name of being for the *citizens*, the government wouldn't allow the hoi polloi to rub shoulders with royalty. Only the most worthy, hand-picked residents would attend.

Many of my clients had wrangled invites to both events, meaning they each needed two different evening gowns. My staff and I were working long nights, but I knew it would all be worthwhile. I dreamed of seeing one of my gowns on the front page of the *Dominion Post*. And not because it was worn by a murder victim with the skirt peeking out from under a blanket.

At the post office, I collected a parcel. We had run woefully short on tiny pearl buttons, and a special order had just arrived from Auckland. Hurrying back, I stood on the edge of the pavement, trying to spot a break in the traffic, so I could dart across the road.

A horn sounded as a motor vehicle swerved around a horse-drawn cart with tall sides. I paused; there would be a chance to cross after the draught horses had ambled past with their covered load. Raised voices and shouts came from behind me. A man shouldered people out of the way as he pushed across the flow of pedestrians.

He seemed young, only in his twenties, and a manual labourer from his rough woollen clothes and the cap pushed back on his head. A battered leather satchel was slung over his shoulder. A dock worker, I assumed, rushing to get his lunch before his break time was over. He held a silver pocket watch in his hand, his thumb rubbing the closed cover as he headed towards me.

My attention was drawn to the item in his hand. The shiny timepiece was at odds with his grubby appearance, but perhaps the watch had belonged to his father. Our paths collided, and he shouldered into me.

He spun and met my gaze. "So sorry Mrs, but I'm late!" He glanced down at the pocket watch and flipped it open. His feet continued to move backwards.

"Look out!" I yelled, his attention fixed on the time-piece and not on where he was going.

He glanced up and stared at me as he continued his path by walking backwards out onto the road. I couldn't look away, as a tram came from the opposite direction to the horse-drawn cart. The tall sides of the covered load had obscured the tram from view. Brakes squealed as the driver tried to halt in time. A sickening thud was followed by a scream from someone nearby.

Or was it me?

I couldn't look away or close my eyes, but my mind went dark to protect myself from the horror of the impact. Thunderous noise crashed over me, and in its wake fell silence. I stared at the spot where the young man had once stood. The tram came to a full stop a few feet along. A foot protruded across the track, the trouser leg pulled up to expose a battered boot. The unfortunate man lay wedged by the front of the tram, his body twisted. The satchel he had carried slung over his shoulder was thrown some distance and the contents scattered on the road.

As one of those closest, I rushed to his side. Blood pooled beneath him. Kneeling, I dropped my parcel and reached my hands out towards him. My brain wanted to ask, *are you all right?* Even though it was obvious he was anything but.

While I struggled with what to say, he raised one hand and gripped mine tight. As though by sheer will, he could cling to life.

"Our...time...is...here..." he stuttered. He pulled on our joined hands, and I leaned closer, assuming he had more to say. But he only let out a faint exhale.

His time was certainly up. Or did he refer to something else? He closed his eyes, and I stared at his firm grip on my hand.

A fading memory drifted through my mind as the man slipped into unconsciousness.

A newspaper was spread over the table. A finger tapped a particular line in the article. 'This is where we do it. No one will be expecting us.'

A murmur of agreement from the men around the table.

'That royal bastard will pay for what they did. He should be held accountable. No more will we wear the British yoke and New Zealand will be free!' the finger pointer yelled.

"Do you mean George, or Edward, the Prince of Wales?" The question rushed from me, regardless of the assembled crowd. I didn't care it wouldn't make sense to anyone clustered around us. If one believed the rumours, George was a royal bastard, or the vision could have referred to our royal visitor. But the lad didn't answer. His head lolled to one side.

His fingers loosened on mine and his hand dropped back to his chest.

The tram driver had left his vehicle and stood beside me. He removed his cap and clutched it to his chest. "He stepped right in front of me! I couldn't stop in time."

I knelt back on my heels as a chill swept over me. What did I do? The man could have shared a memory of a conspiracy plot, or a scene from a movie. My gift didn't come with subtitles that gave me a clear context of what I saw. Then a horrid realisation swept over me as I stared at him.

His face was the one I saw in the snippet of memory I gleaned from Bridget the night of my showing.

The air whooshed from my lungs, and a tingle erupted along my arms. I couldn't recollect another instance where my gift showed me the same or similar memory lifted from two different people. Was this one important? The angry words weren't aimed at our George, king of the streets, as he never wrapped any New Zealander in chains of servitude.

But the man was dead now, so surely any threat to Prince Edward was likewise extinguished. Except he hadn't been the only man around the table. Nor did his voice match the one who had spoken as he tapped the article.

Whistles sounded and the pounding of feet heralded the arrival of a policeman at the scene of the accident.

"Is he dead?" a male voice said from behind me.

"Let's have a look at him then, madam, if you don't mind moving," another bystander said.

Turning, a policeman stood next to me, staring down at the man.

"Of course." I gathered up my parcel and rose to unsteady feet.

The policeman knelt and placed his fingers against the man's neck. After a long moment, he let out a sigh and stood. "Nothing to be done for him."

The tram driver had a blanket under his seat, and he draped it over the dead man's head and shoulders. The passengers descended from the tram since it wouldn't be moving for some time, and either continued on foot or looked for another tram on a different line.

"Are you all right, love?" An elderly lady rested a gnarled hand on my forearm.

I drew a deep breath. "I will be after a cup of tea. Thank you for asking."

"You might want to wash your hands." She gestured with her head.

Only now did I stare down. One hand was bloody, and my skirt was dusty from where I knelt in the road.

"Yes. I shall." There was nothing I could do, and

yet I couldn't leave the scene. I returned to the sheltering eave of the shops and watched. The policeman and another man picked up the scattered belongings and returned them to the satchel. The bag was then placed on the dead man's chest to go with him. Soon, an ambulance rumbled along the road and halted by the tram. Two men jumped out and set out a stretcher. I averted my gaze as they extricated the poor man. Only when the doors swung shut and the vehicle headed down the road did the spell the accident had cast over me break.

With sadness weighing my every step, I crossed the road and headed up Plimmer Steps. Etty sat at the long curved main desk when I climbed the stairs to my atelier. My ladies took turns doing handwork at the desk, to ensure any customer was greeted immediately and not left standing.

"There you are. You've been ever so long. We were getting worried about you," Etty said.

"There was an accident," I murmured.

"Blimey!" Etty rose and came around the side of the desk. "Is that your blood?"

"No. A young man stepped in front of a tram, and I was beside him. He grabbed my hand as he..." *Died.* I had held his hand as he slipped from this life to whatever lay beyond.

I placed the parcel on the desk. "I shall go and wash up." Shrugging out of my coat, Etty took it from me so I didn't transfer blood to the wool.

"I'll put the kettle on. You could do with a strong cup of tea."

In the bathroom, I scrubbed the blood and dirt from my hands. The cool water ran over my skin, and I watched it swirl down the drain. Words flitted through my mind. *I'm late. Our time is here.* The young man staring at the expensive pocket watch. Just like the rabbit in *Alice in Wonderland.* Except he didn't disappear down a dark hole. Or I suppose he did if you considered death a sort of dark tunnel.

When I emerged, Etty had made me a mug of tea and pressed it into my hands. Then she insisted I sit in front of the tall window with its watery sunlight while I collected myself. Thanking my assistant, I decided to immerse myself in work instead. My brain needed to be busy, not dwelling on the horrid event.

"Has Miss Belmont booked for her final fitting?" I had decided the young woman was my third favourite client, after Mrs Cooper and Mrs Taylor. She delighted in giving me free rein to design her gowns, as long as we stuck with her preferred colours, and I wasn't too adventurous.

"Yes. Monday at one p.m.," Etty said. "You have a full schedule of bookings over the next two weeks."

For Miss Belmont to wear to the ball at Government House, we had settled on a deep pink silk underdress. A sheer overlay was beaded and made the silk shimmer as though it were covered in raindrops. The gown for the Citizens Ball was a pale pink, edged in silver tassels. I had poached Mrs Mac, the Cricket's costume designer, to help with all the beading. The older woman was a genius with beading and sequins, and she appreciated having work she could do at home while tending her war-injured son.

The prince stepping onto New Zealand soil would create a frenzy in our country. In Wellington, we were somewhat removed from the hysteria, but the local paper already ran photos from Auckland of where the ship would berth and the roads the prince would travel. People practised waving their Union Jack flags, and many speculated whether they might receive a royal handshake. In three weeks' time, he would journey down New Zealand to Wellington.

I swallowed a few more fortifying sips of tea. "Let us crack on. We have much to do to be ready for next week."

I lost myself in ensuring the gown was perfect for the final fitting, and it was only when Etty tapped my shoulder that I realised it was time to shut up for the night.

Chapter Three

At home, I sat at the table and helped Theo with his homework. His joy at starting school had turned into horror that he was supposed to do *work* at *home*! I hid my smile. Wait until he discovered what awaited him after school and the horrors of adulthood and bills that needed paying. Mathematics was woven into wood-working projects Theo did with Dad, and his reading was coming along nicely. It made my heart swell to see him curled up next to his Poppa as they read a war story of dashing adventures.

That night, I pushed my dinner around the plate and let the chatter between Dad and Theo drift around me.

"Are you going to eat that or just play with it?" Dad waved his fork at me from across the table.

I set down my cutlery. "Sorry, I don't seem to be hungry, and my mind is a thousand miles away." That wasn't entirely correct. My thoughts were more like

400 miles away in Auckland, where the handsome prince would soon dazzle the population.

Dad cleared his throat. "It's not easy seeing someone die in front of you. Your mind keeps trying to fix it by doing something different, but you can't go back in time."

"Who died?" Theo asked.

I had told Dad what had happened as soon as I got home, needing his silent hug to lift away some of the pain. "A man stepped in front of a tram today, and it couldn't stop in time."

Despite his tender years, Theo knew all about death. It had taken his father before he was born, and talk of it had permeated every day for most of his young life.

He screwed up his face. "That was silly. You always look before you cross the road."

"Yes, you should," I agreed. The man had been distracted, staring at a timepiece, his back to the traffic. Something had pressed on his mind, and I couldn't shake the image my gift lifted from his skin in his dying moments.

That royal bastard will pay...

Gooseflesh erupted along my arms, and I rubbed it away. "I wonder who he was."

The attending policeman had collected the scattered belongings, but from what I overheard, there was nothing with a name or any way to identify him. Only an apple, a pair of pliers, some coils of wire, and a worn pack of playing cards.

So many of our lads died on foreign soil, and some were buried without anything to mark their resting place. Everybody deserved a name on their grave. A person shouldn't die on a Wellington street and have less to mark his passing than a soldier killed in Gallipoli or Passchendaele. I couldn't give a name to those men in their unmarked graves, but I could do something about the fellow who breathed his last while I held his hand.

"I'm sure someone will claim him. Didn't you say you thought he came from the wharves?" Worry wrinkled the corner of Dad's eyes.

"Yes. He was dressed like a wharfie and came from that direction." But it was only a guess. The man could have been a worker from any business along the bustling waterfront. Or perhaps someone who worked with electrics, given the contents of his satchel.

"Then someone will have reported him missing from his afternoon shift. The newspapers will have the story tomorrow, and that will alert anyone who expected him home tonight." Dad continued with his dinner.

I picked up my fork and stabbed a piece of mutton. Reading a newspaper article would be a horrid way to learn your husband or brother had passed. Somewhere across town, had someone cooked a dinner that sat cooling on the table, waiting for the man to walk through the door?

After dinner, we did the dishes, and Theo played on the floor with his wooden motorcars. Triumph the hamster was tucked up asleep in his palatial run outside, and I told my son not to disturb the little creature as hamsters didn't like night-time races. Instead, he placed tin soldiers in the driver's seat and made engine noises as they circled the rug.

Dad made cocoa, and I tidied away my belongings. Fatigue had sapped my limbs when I came home, and I had tossed my coat over the spare chair. Picking up the bright blue wool coat, I gave it a once over. Only now wondering if any spots of blood had stained the fabric while I knelt by the dying man.

As I turned the garment this way and that, and ran my hand along the hem, something about it struck me as odd. One side seemed to weigh more than the other. In my distracted state, I hadn't noticed it until now. Had I been carrying one of Theo's toys in my pocket all day? Sliding my hand into the right-hand side pocket, my fingers closed around cool metal. Pulling the object out, I held a silver pocket watch.

The same watch that had distracted the man and caused the fatal accident. My brain tried to determine how the timepiece came to be in my coat. Could the man have dropped it and, in my confused state, I had picked it up and placed it in my pocket? Or did he place it there deliberately while I knelt at his side?

I turned it over in my hands. It was a beautiful piece, or once had been. A deep impression about a half inch in diameter scarred the back. The front was etched with a circular pattern and an ornate motif in the middle. The name *Hector Dalton* was carefully engraved in the centre. Around the edge was tiny metal beading in three rows.

"What have you got there, love?" Dad asked as he placed two mugs of cocoa on the table.

I turned and held up the pocket watch by the short length of chain. "It's the watch that so distracted the young man. Somehow, it ended up in my pocket. There's a name on the front. Do you think it's him?" I passed the item over to Dad.

My father turned it over in his grasp and rubbed his thumb over the hole, the edges either worn smooth or filed down. "This is a bullet hole."

"Really?" I stared at the watch with renewed fascination.

"You hear stories of men who were shot and something in a pocket saved them. Normally it's a small book, the bullet penetrating the pages. Or a flask that ends up dented like this. I'd not heard of a pocket watch taking a bullet, but this certainly looks like one." He turned the watch over and opened the front, then held it up to his ear. "It doesn't go. The impact must have damaged the mechanism."

That didn't make any sense. If the pocket watch didn't keep time, why was the young man staring at it so intently?

Dad inserted his thumbnail under the seam at the back, but it didn't budge. Next, he used a knife and gently slid the blade into the gap. With a twist of his wrist and a bit of encouragement, the back came open. "There's an inscription, hard to read around the hole, but it's *to my*, something, *Hector*. Son, husband, maybe? Then another few words with the middle missing that I think refer to some occasion and a year—1887. If the chap who died was only young, this might have been his father's and passed down to him. This Hector chap might have dodged one bullet, but his relative ran into another."

"He kept it for some reason," I said, "even if it didn't keep time. At the least, it might be a clue to his identity if no one has claimed his body. Either way, I shall return it in the morning." Although I wasn't sure where to hand it in. Since the man was deceased, I couldn't leave it sitting on his bedside cabinet by his hospital bed. It should be in his satchel with his other things. At the least, I could make enquiries.

"Or the fellow might have nicked it from a pawn shop and was making his escape when he realised it didn't go," Dad added.

That was a less helpful scenario. Whatever the significance of the pocket watch, it didn't belong to me. I would take it to the police station and they could ferret out the true owner.

Monday morning, I scanned the newspaper for more information about the horrible incident. Page three had a small article about the terrible accident that had taken the man's life and finished with a call for any information about the man who lay unidentified in the city morgue.

"How sad," I murmured as I chewed the end of toast.

"What's sad?" Dad asked from across the table.

"That chap who died Friday still has no name. If he came from the wharves, they surely would have heard of the accident and realised he was missing. The article is asking for anyone with information to aid his identity to come forward." The pocket watch would definitely help since it had a name. Assuming it belonged to someone in the man's family. "I'll take the watch to the police station before work."

The newspaper reporter gave the name of the policeman trying to identify the man. The threat against the prince in his memory flitted across my mind. Could I give it any weight, though? It could have been something said in the heat of the moment. I couldn't imagine anyone wanting to mar the royal visit with violence.

But two visions, from two people, about the same thing? How I wished I were the sort of person who could sweep aside such matters as not being of my concern. Whatever ran through my veins and made me different, seemed to want me to interfere in all types of things to set them to rights.

After breakfast, I walked Theo to the Thorndon School and watched him rush off excitedly to play with his fellow new students before the bell rang. I leaned on the brick wall surrounding the playground. For the first week, he had allowed me to walk him to class and help him hang his satchel. Then, once familiar with the routine, he declared himself too big for my help, and I was abandoned at the school gate.

An odd combination of pain and love flared through my chest as I watched the boys play. My body contained a fierce love for my son and part of me wanted to hold on to the child forever. But as he grew, he would snip each apron string that bound us together. Each cut would create a scar on my heart that time would stitch closed. Pride for the man he would become would always be tempered by the pain of losing the little boy who held my hand so tight.

Yet I would never stop the process or wish it any other way. How strong women were—we bore children and poured all our love into raising them, knowing we would lose them. With the sound of laughter in my ears, I carried on down the hill and towards the police station.

Inside, the place bustled with policemen and civilian workers going back and forth. A ruffian was pushed along a corridor by a burly man in dark blue. The clatter of typewriters and the ring of a telephone filled the air. I approached the front desk. An aging policeman with mutton chop sideburns from the Victorian era stared at me over the gold rims of his spectacles.

"What can I do for you, madam?" he asked.

As I reached into my bag, a familiar voice came from behind me. "Can I be of assistance, Mrs Devine?"

I curled my fingers around the timepiece and then let go as I turned. "Good morning, Detective Archer. It's about the poor chap who stepped in front of the tram on Friday."

"You knew him?" The detective arched one dark eyebrow.

"No. I was standing next to him. He bumped into me and that was why he didn't see the tram. If only I had grabbed hold of his jacket, I might have stopped him." Guilt sucked all the moisture from my throat and my tongue pushed the words forth. Would I ever stop feeling responsible for his death? If we hadn't collided, he wouldn't have been distracted. If I had snatched hold of the strap of his satchel, I might have arrested that fatal backwards step.

"Why don't we go somewhere quieter, and you can tell me what happened?" The detective gestured down the corridor.

"I don't want to take up your time." My fingers tightened on my bag. The last time I had been in a room here with the detective, he had questioned me about the involvement in the death of a showgirl.

"I think this warrants my time." He nodded to the policeman at the front desk.

"Thank you," I murmured and fell into step beside Joseph's superior officer.

Along the corridor, he pushed open the door to his office and gestured for me to precede him. I plonked myself down in a chair before his desk, the swirl of emotions dampening my mood.

"You were not responsible for his death." Detective Archer took the seat next to me, tugging the legs of his trousers up a few inches before lowering his frame.

"I could have stopped him. I keep seeing that moment as he stepped backwards." My hands tightened on the handles of my bag. In my mind, I lunged and grabbed...*anything*...that would halt his course of action. The tram might still have grazed his body, but he might have survived.

"We cannot take on responsibility for the actions of others." His voice had a low, comforting tone.

"Even if their actions are our fault?" I searched his dark gaze, seeking any sign he also blamed me.

"I was a captain during the war. Every time I had to send men out on missions, I knew some might not return. I did all I could to give them the best chance. Even when my superiors forbade it, I led from the front. I couldn't stay safe in the trenches and send those lads over the top into enemy territory. I asked nothing of them that I was not prepared to do myself. And yet..." He sighed and his eyes became unfocused as memories tugged him back to the battlefield.

"Surely you don't hold yourself responsible for the deaths of soldiers under your command. We were at war." What a burden to take on. How did he manage to breathe even, if every death pressed on him?

"You would absolve me of responsibility when my direct command caused the death of a man, while you take on the guilt of another's moment of inattention and a terrible accident?" The sadness in his eyes was tempered with a flicker of humour.

When he said it like that, it made no sense. All I knew was the moment was carved deep in my mind, and I kept trying to alter the course of events. "He held my hand as the spark in his eyes was extinguished by death."

Chapter Four

Detective Archer removed the navy pocket square from his jacket and offered it to me. I hadn't even realised I was crying. With a thankful nod, I took the linen and dabbed at my eyes. My tears made dark patches in the soft fabric.

"You must think me a silly woman," I whispered, as I refolded the handkerchief and handed it back.

He took the square and laid it on the desk surface. "No. I think you are a caring person who was affected by being at the poor lad's side in his last moments. Don't underestimate the comfort your presence would have given him. None of us wants to die alone."

The sadness in his tone made me glance up, but his face was turned away as he straightened a sheet of paper on his desk. Turning his words over in my mind lifted a little of my guilt. However reluctantly, I had been there as a witness when the man breathed his last.

I opened my bag and extracted the damaged pocket

watch, holding it out on my palm. "He was staring at this, then...afterwards...he must have slipped it into my coat pocket. I didn't notice until I got home. There is a name engraved on the lid. I thought it might help identify the young man."

"I shall pass it to the officer searching for his next of kin." With a gentle touch, he took the timepiece from me. Turning it over, he rubbed a thumb about the bullet hole.

"My dad thought it might have saved someone's life, taking a bullet meant for him." As soon as I said the words, I realised the irony if the watch had saved the lad's father, only to snatch the son's life.

"I had a man under me who was shot in the chest. We thought he was done for, what with the dark liquid staining the front of his coat. Turned out, the bullet hit his flask in his top pocket. It saved his life. Spilt the rum in it though, which upset him terribly." He huffed a soft laugh at the memory.

I swallowed, nerves crawling over my skin like a procession of ants. There was another reason for my visit to the police station, and I needed to unburden myself. I could not think of a better confessional than Detective Archer's office. But if even I thought the idea ridiculous, how to word it without appearing mad? "In those last moments, when I held his hand, the man said... he said *our time is here* and..." I had to pause and ask the man's spirit for forgiveness for the alteration of the truth about to pass my lips, "*that the royal...*" here I stumbled for another word as I couldn't say *bastard* in the policeman's hearing, *"...prince would pay for what they did. He should be held accountable."*

I couldn't meet the detective's gaze. Technically, the words weren't a lie. I had heard them spoken, but they didn't pass the lips of the unknown victim of the accident but from another.

Silence lay heavy over the room for a long minute. "You think this individual may have represented a threat to Prince Edward?"

I let out a sigh and stared at the pocket watch. "I don't know. It seems silly now that I say it out loud. He could have been referring to anything. But he implied New Zealand would be free. I know there are those who agitate against the monarchy and who think New Zealand should be a republic, like America. I would never forgive myself if there were more to his words, and I said nothing."

The detective leaned back in his chair and made a humming noise in the back of his throat. "With the prince about to step onto New Zealand soil, the constabulary are vigilant in finding any threats to his safety. We are aware of a small group of activists who might intend harm. I will dig a little deeper into this man's background once we have a name for him. Thank you for bringing this to me, Mrs Devine."

With the weight lifted from my conscience, I left the matter with the detective and carried on to my work premises.

Once I hung up my coat in my office, my day was a blur of activity, colour, and gorgeous fabrics. We barely had time for lunch, but I made sure all the girls had a break and washed their hands thoroughly before touching the gowns again.

"How is your brother, Etty, after recent events?" I asked as I stopped at the cutting table on my way back to my office. My assistant's younger brother, Patrick, had become tangled with a hate-fuelled group that saw him land in trouble with the law. And more terrifying for him, with his sister.

Etty let out a sigh, and her hands tightened on the shears, poised to cut around the weighted pattern pieces. "That daft lad just doesn't learn. Now he's being all patriotic and hanging out with other Irish lads who are all hot under the collar about Home Rule. Not that it helps that it's all Da and his mates talk about these days. One of them, Mr Griffin, was lucky to escape with his life after the Easter Rising in 1916. He scarpered from Ireland all the way to New Zealand with his family after that."

"Is there much that can be done for Ireland from here?" From other conversations with Etty, I knew a little about the struggle of the Irish to govern them-selves. The British government had passed an Act in 1914, to allow Ireland limited governance. Then the outbreak of the Great War meant the new law wasn't implemented. The Easter Rising of 1916 was an unsuc-cessful attempt to wrest back that control. Since one war ended, another had erupted with the Irish Inde-pendence movement.

Etty laid one hand on the stiffened paper as she

followed the outline with the sharp scissors. "They petition politicians here, to whisper in the ears of the British ones. Then they are always writing letters back to the home country. Now they are muttering that the royal visit is their chance to be heard. I suspect Patrick and his mates will be waving placards or yelling slogans, and hoping that the newspapers will take their photograph and send it around the world."

I wondered if the dead man might have been Irish. That would explain what I saw. He and his associates might have been organising such a protest. Although, thankfully, I didn't recollect Patrick's face in the fading memory. Etty's brother struck me as a lad who was lost in life and searching for a cause to believe in. Coupled with his youth and, dare I say it, a dash of naiveté, he was following the wrong sorts who were leading him into unsavoury spots. So far, our attempts to slip him under Joseph's steadying influence were unsuccessful. But Etty and I were undeterred.

"I suspect the police will move on those lads quickly if they try staging a protest." For once, I was happy to leave such matters in the capable hands of Detective Archer.

My assistant added the fabric pieces to a pile at the edge of the cutting table. "Serves them right if both Patrick and Da get locked up for causing a nuisance. You would think the old men would know better, but I swear they are worse than the young ones."

"I don't believe age and maturity necessarily go hand in hand with men," I murmured.

"I wonder why Mr Griffin came all this way when he wants to be back amongst it in Ireland. You should see the colour of red he goes when he gets all worked up about it." Etty cast around the room and pounced on a small scrap of red silk. "He looks just like this!" She waved the snippet.

"It's his homeland. I don't know if you can ever sever that sort of tie. If I were sent to live on the other side of the globe, I'm sure I would miss New Zealand." I marvelled at the fortitude of people who braved weeks in the vessels to come so far south and start a new life.

Etty shrugged. "I'm from there, and I don't feel any particular need to return. Not that I remember much. What I do, looks a lot like New Zealand. Green fields. Sheep. Men getting drunk and causing trouble." She met my gaze across the table and humour simmered in their hazel depths.

"Perhaps the world is not as large as I think it is, and we are all more similar than I realised." No matter where you went in the world, what language you spoke, or the accent you had, we were all the same deep inside.

"Let me know as soon as Miss Belmont arrives for her final fitting." The chatter of the women rang in my ears as I retreated to the quiet of my office. The appointment book was full and even though it was only autumn, my thoughts turned to spring and summer. Those at the forefront of society would need the latest fashion to wear as soon as the seasons changed, which meant preparing months in advance. I had to order fabrics and trims from England and Europe, to have on hand to show clients alongside the sketches.

There were other aspects of running a business that weren't any fun at all. Like ordering supplies and paying the bills. "But we have to take the good with the bad," I whispered one of Dad's sayings under my breath as I completed a form to mail off to England.

I was squinting at a column of numbers and trying to remember my four times tables when Etty rapped on my door. "Miss Belmont is here for her final fitting."

"Brilliant. Is her gown in the fitting room?" I tucked the basket beside my desk.

"Yes, it's waiting in number one." Etty grinned. We were both excited to see the final result on our client. We had spent days, or it certainly felt like it, to get the drape just right.

Ensuring I had my pin cushion tied to my wrist, just in case, I hurried out to greet the wealthy young woman. I found Miss Belmont standing by the curved wooden desk conversing with Miss Novikoff, the gloomy and disapproving friend from my showing the previous week. It wasn't unusual for a young socialite to bring a friend to fittings. Their gossip drifting over the top of my head as I fussed with a seam or hemline.

"Miss Belmont, Miss Novikoff, it is lovely to see you both. If you would follow me, please." I gestured to the first fitting room and held the door open while they passed inside. While generous in size, the room was getting a little snug with four of us in there and the draped dress form. The pale pink chiffon from the train peeking out from under its sheet.

Miss Belmont practically squealed in excitement at the glimpse, and we hadn't whipped off the cover yet. Her friend dropped to a chair in the corner and gazed around. I could see her mentally comparing my little fitting room to whatever grand, mirror-lined room she was used to in Russian palaces.

"I hope you don't mind, Mrs D, but Leena here has decided she wants a gown to wear to the Citizens Ball. She thought she could have a fitting while I was here," Miss Belmont said after she emerged from behind the screen and twirled in front of the mirror.

I opened my mouth to protest, or say something terribly rude, and then snapped it shut. I exchanged a startled look with Etty and then considered what I could say that wouldn't antagonise a wealthy potential client.

"I am flattered, Miss Novikoff, that you wish me to design you a gown. However, we simply don't have time. Our books are overflowing as it is with final fittings. I am afraid I couldn't start a gown until after the royal visit."

"There was a red dress during your little show. That will be acceptable with some changes." She waved a hand and sniffed, as though she were doing me a great favour to deign to wear one of my little designs.

The red gown in question would undoubtedly look marvellous with her darker colouring. The Russian woman would be a stunning temptress. If I had the time.

"My gown is perfect, Mrs D. There's not a single thing you need to tweak. We would have time, wouldn't we, for Leena to try that red number on?" Miss Belmont stopped her twirling and beseeched me with her large blue eyes.

I wavered at her imploring expression and could only imagine that men were putty in her hands.

"I'll fetch it, Mrs Devine, while you assist Miss Belmont," Etty offered.

Since I was ambushed and outnumbered, I had no choice. "Very well, Etty. But we have very little time for any alterations, Miss Novikoff. But let us see what we can do in what remains of Miss Belmont's fitting session."

Etty retrieved the red silk gown, while I removed the pink chiffon from my client. One woman swapped places with the other behind the screen. My assistant carried away the finished gown to wrap in tissue paper and place in a box for Miss Belmont to take away with her.

Miss Novikoff emerged from behind the screen, whose stretched fabric was painted with wading cranes in colours that matched the fitting room. She stepped onto the raised platform before the mirror. While my resentment smouldered in a corner, I had to admit that objectively the gown didn't just fit her; she embodied it.

Of a deceptively simple Grecian-inspired design, the red silk wrapped around the wearer's body. The bodice was high in the front and scandalously low in the back and pooled in a simple train.

"It needs...sparkle." Miss Novikoff raised her hands and then flung them apart, wriggling her fingers like stars falling to earth.

"It would be monstrously difficult to bead now the gown is finished. Not to mention that beading is slow and time-intensive work." Nor did I want to ruin the simple design by scattering beads over it.

"I will pay for your time. Money is no issue." Again with the dismissive hand, as though any amount of money could manufacture more time in the day.

"I appreciate your generosity, Miss Novikoff, but there are only so many hours in a day, and my seamstress, who does the specialist beadwork, is already busy." Not entirely true, as we had almost finished all the commissions for the royal visit and Mrs Mac's workload had eased.

The Russian huffed and narrowed her gaze at me in the mirror.

You're a fool, Grace Sullivan, I said to myself in Dad's voice. I picked up the modest train and gestured to the drape at the back. "We could, possibly, bead the neckline, back, and perhaps make a garland of beads that would nestle among the draping at the back."

Miss Novikoff huffed again and turned this way and that. "That would be acceptable."

I was *so* pleased that piling a horrible amount of work onto my staff was acceptable to her. Then I pushed my internal rant to one side and considered the gown with a keen eye. My mind examined every seam and drape. Grabbing the first pin, I set about making minute adjustments that would take the fit from perfect to...divine.

Etty fetched a tray of sample beads we used to show clients. After the demanding young woman had changed back into her day clothes, we considered the embellishments to add to the gown. In a short time, we settled on three hues of iridescent red, with a matte black to highlight the sheen of its companions. While Miss Novikoff's abrupt manner rubbed me the wrong way, she certainly knew her mind and made decisions quickly.

"I will make the adjustments to the gown and have the beading done in the next week. We shall try to find a final fitting for you before the ball," I said as I showed the two women out.

Miss Belmont placed a hand on my arm as her companion started down the stairs. "Thank you, Mrs D," she whispered. "I know many people don't like Leena, but there's a heart of gold under the prickly armour."

Somehow I doubted that, but I would hold the Russian to her promise of more than adequately compensating me for the late nights we would have to work. Which reminded me that she had swanned off without paying a deposit. I could hear the lecture from Dad in my ear already.

Chapter Five

Late that afternoon, as the light dimmed, my ladies packed up and called out their goodnights as they hurried to their homes. I circled the room, draping cotton over the gowns to protect them from any stray dust motes that might try to land on them overnight. As I stood at the door and surveyed the workroom, I allowed myself a moment of satisfaction at how my business had grown. For a shop girl who discovered she was pregnant after her man shipped out to war, I hadn't done too badly for myself.

I clicked off the light and wandered back through the building, locking the door securely on my way out. I paused on the step and wrapped my coat tighter around me. Rain had begun to fall, and the wind whipped droplets against my face. It would be an unpleasant walk home.

Light flashed from the Lambton Quay end of Plimmer Steps and a motor rumbled.

"Grace!" a familiar voice called out.

Never had I been more grateful for Joseph and his horrid contraption. Hurrying down the lane, my cousin straddled his motorcycle at the end, where he had been waiting for me.

"Thank you, Joseph." I hitched my skirt, not caring who saw my exposed knees, and climbed on behind him.

"The man killed by the tram has been identified. His name was Adam Dalton. Detective Archer has passed on the pocket watch to his brother and thought you would like to know," he said as I wrapped my arms around his torso.

Then he opened the throttle and the chance to converse was snatched away as the motorcycle roared up the road. That was thoughtful of the detective to pass on the information. Pieces shifted inside me when I thought of the quiet and intense man. Perhaps my initial impression of him, coloured by being a murder suspect and him examining every aspect of my life, had been overly harsh.

The trip home was short, and Joseph took the brunt of the weather. As I clambered off the motorcycle, a pang shot through my heart for the lad I once thought was nothing more than a bumbling oaf. I rested a hand on his shoulder. "I appreciate you coming to get me."

He shrugged. "You might have changed your name, but you're still a Sullivan on the inside, and we look out for each other." Then he steered the Triumph towards his home.

Yes, I thought to myself; we look out for each other. Which is exactly why I am going to chip away at the armour you built around yourself during the war. Once I have made a hole big enough, I intend to sneak somebody in there to make you laugh again. I never realised what a tricky mission that would be or the thickness of his armour. But having inherited Dad's stubbornness, I refused to give up.

The next few days passed like every other—in a blur of manic work. Thursday morning, I sat at the table and savoured my tea and toast. After breakfast, I walked Theo to school and then I hurried to Plimmer Steps and the warmth of my space. The autumn chill grew more pervasive and the threat of rain more frequent. After checking on everyone's progress, I made a cup of tea and sat at my slanted desk under the tall and narrow window.

I had an idea for a new dress for Mrs Taylor using the autumnal print I had found. As I sketched ideas, Etty knocked on my open door.

"Yes?" I glanced around, the pencil poised in my hand.

"I know we're awfully busy, but could I possibly take an hour or two off this afternoon?" Worry crinkled her brow.

"Of course. We'll manage for a little while without you." She wouldn't have asked if it weren't important, and more than once I had left Etty in charge while I took care of urgent business.

Relief smoothed the lines around her eyes. "Thank you, Mrs Devine. It's the funeral of Adam Dalton today. My friend, Bridget, was stepping out with him, and I promised I'd go with her. She's ever so cut up about him dying."

Dalton. The name bounced around in my head until it hit the target. "Oh." The breath whooshed out of my lungs. Joseph had told me that was the man whose hand I held while he breathed his last. His body had been identified by his brother.

"I didn't realise the other day when you came back straight after..." Etty's hushed words trailed off into nothing.

We stared at one another, lost in the terrible memory. My relief that the man had been identified butted up against sadness at such a tragic loss of life. For a moment, I considered if I should attend the funeral, but I didn't want any upset family members laying the blame at my feet. At a previous funeral, a distraught mother had all but pointed at my head and yelled, *murderer!* In that instance, I knew I was innocent of the charge. I couldn't pretend a lack of involvement in Mr Dalton's demise.

I suspected the day he died would haunt me until the end of my days. When I couldn't sleep at night, those few seconds played over and over in my head. He bumped against me, turning to apologise. His foot continued backwards, unaware of the tram hidden by the passing cart. If only I had snatched at his jacket, or the satchel around his shoulder, and stopped him.

I twisted the pencil between my fingers. "Please tell Bridget, and Mr Dalton's family, how terribly sorry I am. I wish I had stopped him. Somehow."

Etty shook her head. "He always had his head in the clouds, that one. Adam wasn't from Ireland, but being around our families, he followed what was happening over there. He used to say you didn't have to be Irish to stand up against injustice when you see it, and that the British Empire needed a good prune to get rid of the rot. I used to wonder if he just said it so that Mr Griffin would let him court Bridget."

Adam Dalton's last moments and the shared memory drifted through my mind. It made more sense now. He must have been organising a Home Rule protest. That brought back to my mind Etty's worry about her brother being involved.

"Was he involved in the same protests as Patrick that you were telling me about?" Sometimes I thought I should be taking notes about the potential troubles young men got into, so I could refer to them when Theo reached a similar age.

Etty blew out a sigh. "Bridget said Adam was planning something, but she didn't know what. Our staunch Irish lads aren't keen on letting anyone who might be English in their group, so I doubt he was organising anything with that lot. Patrick would know, though. I keep hoping he'll see sense and stay out of trouble, but it's difficult when Da and Mr Griffin encourage him."

I wished I could do more to ease Etty's worries about her brother. Our plan to tuck him under Joseph's wing had yet to bear fruit. "I take it Patrick's attitude towards the constabulary still hasn't changed?"

Etty rolled her eyes. "No. Those couple of times we organised for him to come here to escort me home, Constable Sullivan fetched you in his uniform. You should have heard Patrick mutter all the way home about coppers. I wonder if he'd talk about motorcycles more freely if your cousin was in his regular clothes."

An idea occurred to me that might bring the two parties together. "Anzac Day is only a few days away. Perhaps we could meet up afterwards? Joseph will be in a different uniform and will most likely have his Triumph tucked away somewhere handy."

My assistant brightened up. "That would be brilliant, Mrs Devine. Patrick loves to talk to soldiers about the war, and it might be the chance we need to get him over his silly distrust of the police."

How odd that Patrick disliked a blue uniform but viewed a khaki one with respect. I would have to ask what he thought of the navy since their uniform was also a shade of blue. "Well, we can sort out the finer details tomorrow. Please convey my condolences to Mr Dalton's mother and father this afternoon."

Sadness dropped over Etty's hazel eyes as she recalled the purpose of her visit to my office. "Oh, both his parents have passed. Their father died during the war and then the influenza took his mother. It was only Adam and his older brother left."

Grief speared through me for a sibling now bereft of his entire family. "How sad. Take as much time as your friend needs this afternoon. We'll manage without you, somehow."

"Thank you." She flashed me a quick smile and left my office.

Friday night after dinner, and once we'd done the dishes, I curled up in the armchair by the window, my cocoa resting on the windowsill. On my lap, I spread the newspaper and devoured the article about Adam Dalton's funeral the previous afternoon.

There was little more detail than what Etty had shared. His poor mother had waved her husband and both sons off to war. I couldn't imagine what she felt as their vessel pulled away, wondering if she would see any of them again. Her husband did not survive the war, fortunately, both sons did. Then Mrs Dalton fell victim to the influenza pandemic that claimed millions of lives around the world. Poor Adam didn't have a bullet with his name on it, but a tram.

The article was accompanied by a photo of the coffin being carried from the church. Mourners gathered around, and I scanned the faces. Etty and Bridget stood to one side. Then another familiar face drew my eye...Miss Fleur Belmont. I wondered how my client knew the deceased. Her gaze didn't seem to be on the coffin as it passed, but on the pallbearer at the front. He had his face cast down and his hat pulled low, so it was impossible to see from the photograph if he were a familiar figure about Wellington.

The doorknob rattled moments before Frank's form filled the space. He shut the door quickly behind him to stop the rain from hurtling in and stomped his feet.

"Hello, Frank," I called out. "The kettle is still warm if you want a cuppa."

"Evening Gracie, Mr Sullivan. Anything stronger than tea on offer?" He shrugged off his overcoat and tossed it over the chair. Then he removed his hat and balanced it on the corner of the chair back.

"Sorry. Your selection is tea, coffee, or cocoa." I unfolded my legs and padded over to the kitchen in my woollen socks. Last winter, I had knitted the orange and yellow striped socks to keep my feet warm while relaxing at home. As I passed the table, I dropped my drink and the newspaper to the surface.

"Coffee, thanks." Frank pulled out a vacant chair and sat.

"What can we do for you this evening, Frank?" Dad scowled over the top of his novel, but the conversation was interrupted by a small projectile hurtling down the stairs.

"Uncle Frank!" Theo rushed into the kitchen,

dressed in striped flannelette pyjamas. He stopped beside his uncle and held out the wooden racing car Dad had made for his hamster. "Wanna race?"

Frank ruffled his nephew's hair. "Maybe another day. Your driver is probably curled up asleep at this hour."

"I think, young man, tonight we shall start *Twenty Thousand Leagues Under the Seas*." Dad levered himself up and plucked a worn book from the small shelf beside his chair.

"Oh, yes, please Poppa." Theo's eyes shone as he said goodnight to his uncle and then presented his cheek to me for a kiss.

"I'll be up to tuck you in later," I murmured.

Dad handed the book to his grandson, who took it as though it were a sacred treasure.

Frank watched the exchange and once the two figures had disappeared from view, he turned to me with a curious look. "What was that about?"

I smiled as I made coffee for Frank. "That is Dad's favourite book of all time, and it is a first edition. He's been promising to read it to Theo for at least a year now."

I set the steaming mug of black coffee in front of Frank and took the chair next to him.

He spun the mug around and around by the handle. "I haven't seen you for a few weeks. Almost feels like you've been avoiding me."

I had, if I were honest. Work being frantic was a

convenient excuse. "Work is crazy, Frank. Every rich woman in Wellington wants a fancy dress and her chance to wow the prince, and there aren't enough hours in the day to keep them all happy."

He reached across the table and took my hand. "I've missed your company."

I let him stroke the inside of my wrist. With my other hand, I picked up the newspaper, folded to expose the article I had been reading. Frank's touch wasn't so distracting that it could pull my mind from the photograph of my client and her focus on the pallbearer as the coffin went by.

Frank's gaze wandered to the article. "Did you know him?"

I smoothed a crinkled corner of the newspaper. "I held his hand as the light faded from his eyes, and he died."

His thumb stilled against my skin. "I'm sorry. I didn't realise you were the one next to him."

"We bumped paths, and I feel as though it was my fault he walked backwards into the path of the tram." How long would it take for the guilt to fade—months, years, or decades? Or when I finally departed this earth and met my maker, would it still be a raw scar?

Frank tapped the article. "I know why this name sounds familiar now. His father was Major Dalton."

I shook my head. "I don't know who that was. Did he do something during the war?"

"You could say that. He was in charge of a campaign that was an utter shambles. A lot of good men died for absolutely no reason or advantage, but at least he died alongside them. Loads of us talked about it at the time. The command given was criminally bad. The army gave him a posthumous dishonourable discharge afterwards." He leaned back in the chair and curled his lip as he recalled whatever gossip swirled in the trenches about Major Dalton.

That sounded terrible. To pursue the dead soldier into the grave, to strip him of his rank and medals. I imagined many mistakes were made during the course of the war. Gallipoli was a terrible failure that saw over 140,000 Allied casualties, including thousands of New Zealand and Australian soldiers, with no ground gained.

"They are a family that has suffered much, and they deserve our sympathy. Etty tells me that Adam was involved with the Home Rule protests and may have planned to stage some disruption of the prince's visit."

"Well, he won't be doing that now, will he?" Frank winked. "How about I take you out next week? Dinner and dancing, instead of you locking yourself away in this cottage." He leaned his forearms on the table.

A part of my brain immediately said *no*. Another part of me stuttered with objections like Joseph's motor-cycle on a cold morning. To lose myself in music for an hour or two. To let my body shake free all the kinks from being bent over my desk. But we had so much work to do. I would bring home garments to hand sew over what was supposed to be our days off.

"Yes. That would be lovely," the treacherous part of me replied while the rational part debated what to do. "But not tomorrow night. We all have to get up early for the dawn parade on Sunday."

Frank grinned, and it lit his amber eyes. "We'll make it Tuesday. I'll pick you up at six."

Chapter Six

SATURDAY AFTERNOON the rain pelted against the windows as I sat in Sam's cosy kitchen and clutched a mug of tea. Theo and Dad were busy in the workshop, while I helped Sam make Anzac biscuits. The biscuits were made with rolled oats, honey, and coconut, and they earned their name as we used to mail them off to our boys overseas. The treats needed to last the long sea voyage, so the mix didn't have any eggs. After the war, we continued to make the biscuits each Anzac Day, which was tomorrow, when we remember the fallen soldiers.

My help in the process was waiting for the delicious-smelling biscuits to come out of the range, so I could eat one. My mind drifted in lazy spirals with the steam rising off my tea.

"Careful there. If you think any deeper, you'll drown in your tea," Sam said as she prepared another tray of biscuits. "What's got you all tied up in knots?"

I let out a sigh and pushed the full mug away from me. "This thing that I can do...with my hands..." I held them up and wriggled my fingers.

"Sewing?" Sam chuckled to herself as she pulled the door open on the range and, using a folded-over tea towel to insulate her hands, carefully took out a tray.

I glared at her turned back and rolled my eyes. Sometimes having a best friend who knew you inside out could be highly annoying. "You know what I mean. You once told me I should practise. To use this...skill... more, to get better at it...but I don't want to. Often, the things I see are personal. It's like peeking in through someone's bedroom window at night." Like when the magic in my veins thrust the image into my head of an older client with her young lover. I still couldn't scrub that intrusion of her privacy from my mind.

Sam placed the tray on the counter and turned to stare at me, a serious glint in her dark eyes. "If you don't want to practise at it to learn better control, what is bothering you about it, then?"

I pursed my lips and waited for the right words to queue up over my tongue. "When I see things...they are like nudges in a direction I am meant to take. Like Theo sneaking something he isn't supposed to have. Or when I saw Mrs Cooper's stolen brooch and that resulted in her offering me the lease on the business. Or when I, or a friend, is accused of murder. The flashes I saw, even if we didn't understand them at the time, eventually led us to who did it."

Sam's lips quirked, and she picked up a knife to

slide the biscuits from the tray to the cooling rack. "But no one was murdered in this instance. The death you witnessed was horrible, but there's no culprit to find. It's not like the tram driver was at fault. Poor man was just doing his job."

Perhaps that was what bothered me this time—the lack of a murder. What sort of person was I becoming, that I needed a gruesome death to make myself feel better about what the trace of magic in my blood showed me? Potentially, harm could befall the prince or those around him if someone was determined enough. But it all felt so vague. "I took the pocket watch Adam Dalton slipped into my coat to the detective and told him a version of what I saw. My role in his death should be done. Yet it seems too easy. And there is this niggle at the base of my brain that says I'm not done, that I'm supposed to do...more."

Up until now, whatever memory the gift latched onto and projected into me propelled me to do something. Even if it was as small as checking Theo's pockets for whatever he shouldn't have. Like Dad's lethally sharp pocket knife. The link between vision and action was also why I was reluctant to practise my ability. I didn't need more to do. What if I started experiencing the problems of all those around me, and was bombarded with things that needed fixing? I was a seamstress, not a psychiatrist, mending everyone's life problems.

Once all the biscuits were off the tray and neatly lined up like little soldiers, Sam used the towel to place the tray in the sink. "What *more* do you want to do with his memory?"

What more could I do? Detective Archer would investigate if any group posed a threat to the royal visitor. Not that his investigation had stopped us from doing our own on previous occasions. "I would never forgive myself if I did nothing, and somebody fired a rifle at the prince sitting in his motorcar as it drove past." A similar incident started the Great War. We didn't need a second war being kicked off in New Zealand.

Excited hysteria already flowed across the country. Today was the day that the dashing young Prince of Wales had arrived Down Under and stepped onto Auckland soil. A special afternoon edition of the newspaper was dominated by grainy photographs of those first few hours. I munched on a warm biscuit while staring at the grinning faces of people frozen in the act of waving their flags as the prince walked along the road. He would spend two days in Auckland before boarding the train to head south. The same train that had been custom-built for the visit of his parents some twenty years earlier.

I offered up a silent prayer to whoever might be listening, that the royal visit would be free of any horrible events or protests. But I could do more than pray. "I want to find out more about the war in Ireland, and these protests Etty's brother is involved in." Saying the words out loud eased the itch a little.

"That's easily done. I've been keeping my ears open

to grumbles from the lads when they come into the bakery. Not all of them are pleased about being led by the nose by England. Many of their families came here to get away from all that aristocratic nonsense and think we should break free like America did." Sam placed four golden biscuits on a plate and set it in front of me.

"I will ask Etty, and maybe see if I can talk to Bridget. She's Etty's friend and was dating Adam." Another face rose to the surface of my mind—Miss Belmont. How was she associated with either the dead man or his family? Next time I saw her, I would drop into our conversation about her attendance at the funeral.

"We have a plan, then. Kostas and Devine are on the case once more, and we shall determine if the Irish lads are going to do something unwise when the prince is in Wellington." Sam waved the spatula at me.

"Since we are working two jobs again, do you think the police force will pay us for investigating?" I grinned at Sam.

"I'll tally the invoices, you hand them over to the detective," Sam said.

That cooled my enthusiasm a little. We would conduct our investigations covertly, without expecting compensation. I took a long drink of my tea and then plucked another biscuit from the pile. Sam was the most brilliant baker and on second thoughts, I was glad she was my best friend.

The itch at the base of my brain settled a little, on hearing that I would dig deeper into whatever Etty's brother was tied up in, and that may have also involved the dead man. I was beginning to wonder if my gift wanted me to save Patrick in particular, as the lad seemed to linger at the edges of whatever trouble I attracted. Thinking of the young man conjured to mind another person who also drifted through my life more and more lately—Detective Archer. I let out a sigh.

"Oh, no, that doesn't sound good. What worry has sprouted in that head now?" Sam pulled out a chair and sat across from me. She took a long drink from her tea mug while she waited for me to start talking.

"What?" I said after the silence extended long enough for me to notice. My mind was fixated on the detective's hands as he twirled his fedora. Was it a nervous habit, or one he did to distract the watcher as he asked his questions?

"You haven't sighed like that since the night Freddie grabbed your hand and pulled you out onto the dance floor." She selected a warm biscuit and bit off one side. "Please tell me you're not pining over Frank?"

I screwed up my face at the thought. "No. I am far too sensible to moon over any man these days. I was thinking about Detective Archer."

Both of Sam's dark eyebrows shot up. "Uh-huh," she murmured with her mouth full.

I needed to say more before my friend leapt to the wrong conclusion that I had lit a torch for the police-man. "Since we are talking about my gift, when I touch Detective Archer, something...odd...happens."

Sam snorted tea, and she coughed. Once she had

regained her breath, she regarded me with mischief sparkling in her dark eyes. "Do I need Mum to have a talk with you?"

I stuck my tongue out at my friend. "Not like that." Was it? The idea stalled my thought processes, and my brain spun faster. I no longer considered him a horrible and mean man out to destroy my life. Events had given me glimpses of the caring individual lurking inside the finely tailored three-piece suit. But what were the new feelings sprouting inside me? Did I...*like* him? No. Nope. No way. I'm not even going to consider the possibility, however remote.

Somehow, I managed to shove that idea back into its stable before it bolted off into the fanciful horizon. "Twice now I've seen memories that weren't memories. Both times it was the same old woman, who I'm guessing is a relative of his. But she talks *to me*."

"Isn't that how your little gift works? You see a person's memories and they talk?" Sam sipped her tea, her full attention on me and my problems. Although I suspected her nose was on alert for when the next batch of biscuits would be done.

How did I explain what happened when my bare skin grazed another and fate, or whatever, decided to yank something from their mind and thrust it into mine? "Normally it's like a play, and I am one of the actors. The script has been written and nothing can be changed. The cinema in my head just...replays it. With Detective Archer and this woman, she responds to what I say in a way that feels...now. I can't help thinking that what happens is only between me and her, and not a memory of the detective."

"Are you worried that digging deeper into what Adam Dalton said to you will bring you into contact with the detective again?" Sam cut to the heart of what worried me.

"Yes. Particularly if we learn anything. I will need to pass it on to the detective. Or I suppose I could ask Joseph to tell him." That should have reassured me. I didn't have to see the detective again, since my cousin could relay any messages. So why did that make the tiniest thread of disappointment wind through me?

Sam ate the last half of the biscuit, and a thoughtful look dropped over her face. When she had finished the treat, she rubbed crumbs from her fingertips. "I admit I didn't like Detective Archer and blamed him for the attacks that happened against my friends. But I was pleasantly surprised when we learned he had been trying to get to the bottom of who was involved. And he arrived in the nick of time to save us all from a beating. So I am inclined to give him another chance. Besides, this is the first time your wriggly hand thing has worked differently on somebody. Maybe there is a reason for that and you're supposed to see more of this weird not-a-memory talking old lady?"

"Or perhaps it means I'm supposed to learn Māori." Although so far I had only learned one word from the old woman—the Māori word for fantail. In the last memory, she had gestured me closer and said a phrase I didn't know.

"She talks to you in Māori?" Sam chuckled. "You don't do anything the easy way, do you?"

I sipped my tea. Life had been a hard road. After Freddie shipped out, I learned I was pregnant. With the help of my amazing friend and family, I established a life as a working mum. Oddly, when we received news that Freddie had been killed in action, it had no impact on my life. While I grieved the man who had a hand in creating my much-loved child, I had been relieved that I would never have to adopt the role of housewife.

But there were many who had it much harder than me. Mrs Mac, my amazing beading maestro, came to mind. She lost her husband. Then her son was terribly wounded and required her to be his full-time nurse. Or lovely George King, who wandered New Zealand with no home after the war. Many people treated him like some sort of pariah because of his far-fetched beliefs about his parentage.

"Life sets me challenges. With each one I overcome, I become a stronger person. This is no different." My words were to reassure myself as much as Sam. We both climbed a mountain strewn with boulders, random rockfalls, and the occasional unexpected crevice. Who knew what we would find at the top if we ever reached it? Perhaps the lesson was to enjoy the view from where we were.

Sam raised an interesting point. My talent showed me memories because I had to do something. The visions of the old woman couldn't be a random chance.

There was a meaning hidden in our interactions. A larger purpose I couldn't see yet. Perhaps the detective's old relative was going to be in some sort of trouble, and I was supposed to help?

There was only one thing that bothered me now. To learn more about the old woman and why we were connected in some magical way, I was going to have to touch the detective's bare skin again.

Chapter Seven

BEFORE DAWN ON SUNDAY MORNING, 25 April, I dressed in the dark and then crossed the hall to rouse my son. Who grumbled and swiped my hands away. "You can stay in bed if you want, but you will miss the parade," I told him.

That galvanised Theo into action. Today was Anzac Day and when we remembered our fallen soldiers. The tradition started in 1916, in honour of the lads of the Australian and New Zealand Army Corps and the ill-fated landing at Gallipoli. The government had yet to make a formal decision about marking the day in legislation, but they couldn't stop the people from showing our respect.

Our lads would march to a temporary cenotaph erected by the Wellington Return Soldiers Association. The wood and plaster structure had been put up on the grass on Parliament grounds at the intersection of Molesworth Street and Lambton Quay. There would be a service and wreaths laid at the foot of the monument.

Theo insisted on marching with his uncles to honour his father. I had initially refused, worried they would lose him in the sea of uniforms. Then, in a rare display of unity, both Frank and Joseph said they would take care of him. How could I refuse, if those warring sides could agree to a ceasefire?

I had made my son a small replica army jacket in the horrid khaki wool our soldiers wore. We pinned Freddie's service medal to the lapel. He didn't have any others, having died within the first year of the war. Dad wore a suit with his medals from the previous century on his chest. As he fussed with their placement, he muttered that his uniform would no longer fit and it must have shrunk in the wash. He wouldn't march but would stand at attention as the navy lads went past.

We gathered out in the street, in the low light just before dawn. I placed Theo's hand in Frank's. Then I leaned closer to Joseph.

"Don't you dare lose your nephew," I whispered as close to his ear as I could reach.

"He'll be safe, I promise." Joseph darted a glance at Frank.

"Safe as houses." Frank grinned and ruffled the top of Theo's head.

For some reason, the vow from Joseph reassured me much more than the same words from Frank's lips.

"Let's go, little soldier. We need to assemble with the others." Frank swung Theo up and onto his shoulders. They would take his motor vehicle down to Courtenay Place. Our men would then march along the streets to Parliament grounds.

"Stay with your uncles and do what you are told," I called out to Theo as they walked off.

My son saluted, and the action tugged at my heart with its echoes of our men leaving Wellington, that long ago day at the wharf.

"Come on, Grace. Let's make our way to Lambton Quay and pick a good spot." Dad had his walking stick today, as he'd be on his wooden foot all day.

Years ago, his foolish pride meant he wouldn't use the stick outside of our home, not wanting to be seen as injured or not as capable as the next man. After toppling over a few times when he was tired or sore, he decided the stick was preferable to the humiliation of being carried home.

Sam and her mum joined us. Mr Kostas had never served, as bakers were considered necessary to maintain essential services and he had been kept at home. War spared him. Influenza had not.

We were subdued as we joined the other people flowing down to the centre of the city. Soon Lambton Quay was lined three deep with people. Reds and orange blushed the sky as though a fire raged on the horizon as the sound of boots and hooves came from further along the road. Cheers heralded the men marching past.

Some of the officers were mounted, riding with one steadying hand on the reins as the horses flinched at the barrage of noise. These equines were not battle-trained. They hadn't been taught how to lie still while a soldier fired his rifle balanced on the saddle. Of the 12,000 horses who went to war alongside our men, only four returned. The fate of those horses ached my heart. They never chose to serve, but they did their best and what a horrid way that trust was repaid.

The next group that marched past us had a familiar figure at the front. Detective Archer, looking smart in his officer's uniform. He had what some would call a *good haul* of medals and bars on his chest.

"I wonder how he did it," Dad murmured from my side.

"By being brave," I replied. What a silly question. In my limited exposure to the policeman, I could see him undertaking daring actions on the battlefield, which saw him awarded with the medals displayed on his jacket. When I gave him the pocket watch, he told me how he didn't expect his men to undertake any risk he wasn't prepared to face himself.

"I meant being a captain of a regular unit. They placed many of the Māori lads in the Māori Battalion." Dad raised his hand and waved to faces he recognised.

My mind froze for a moment, not wanting to confront an uncomfortable truth about our lives. Dad was right. The faces of the soldiers and officers marching past us were various shades of white, or red, having been sunburnt from long days outside. But not many had the darker skin tone of the detective. I spotted a few of them, dotted among their comrades of

British descent, yet only one officer was obviously part-Māori—Captain Archer.

My curiosity wondered how the detective paid for his commission in the army and avoided the segregation of our troops. The British authorities had been reluctant to accept Māori in the army, as they were concerned about giving *the natives* weapons. They seriously believed our boys would turn their rifles on the British soldiers. Or even more ludicrous, they thought the Māori warriors might cause embarrassment by expecting equal treatment with European soldiers. Imagine that. Fighting a war for freedom and expecting equality. The idea made me scoff. Perhaps if they hadn't treated the Māori so terribly, the British wouldn't be so afraid of them.

My thoughts were distracted by Sam elbowing me. "There's Theo."

Frank carried his nephew on his shoulders and given he was already tall, he now appeared like a giraffe among his fellow troops. Theo beamed and waved with both hands at the crowd. Behind them walked Joseph, ready to catch Theo should he topple off his perch.

As the last regiment passed, we fell in behind for the ceremony to come. When the men reached the cenotaph, the troops assembled in neat lines before it. The bystanders made a circle around them. One soldier strode to the front and stood by the monument and played the last post on his trumpet. The haunting notes in the still of the morning caused goosebumps to ripple along my arms.

After the service and laying of the wreaths, the soldiers broke ranks, and we were free to find family and a strong cup of tea or coffee and something hot to eat. Dad and Mrs Kostas stayed in one place, which allowed Sam and me to dart through the crowd to find Theo and his uncles. As I went in the opposite direction from my friend, I encountered Miss Belmont off to one side with a well-dressed group. The familiar form of Miss Novikoff stood beside her. The Russian woman wore a deep red wool coat with brass buttons that made me think of autumn leaves.

"Hello, Miss Belmont. Miss Novikoff," I said as our eyes met.

"Hello, Mrs D. A fine morning, is it not? I can't wait to see that gown you are working away on when it is all done for Leena. What she had planned to wear to the ball is frightfully last year." She playfully batted her friend on the shoulder.

Miss Novikoff's dark eyes narrowed. "What do you expect? Everything in New Zealand is so...provincial. Nothing compares to the luxury we had available to us in Russia."

That dried up the words in my mouth. I worked hard to ensure my creations were every bit as good as those produced in London or Paris. Not to mention I was doing Miss Belmont an incredible favour by squeezing in the last-minute work on a gown for her friend. If she thought it terribly *provincial*, I wasn't sure I would bother to complete it.

"Did you bring any gowns with you from Russia?" I

picked through her comments to find a bright point. This could be a rare chance to handle Russian court dresses and see first-hand their renowned embellishments.

"A few. We came here when war broke out, and I have grown taller since then." Her attention skimmed over my head and to the crowd beyond. She raised her hand and gestured to someone behind me.

Pre-war fashion was quite different from what we crafted after the war. Since Miss Novikoff had fled Russia, war and revolution had devastated the country. The newspapers said it was on the brink of economic collapse. New Zealand might be terribly uncivilised, but I also doubted there were too many balls to attend in St Petersburg or Moscow these days.

Miss Belmont rolled her eyes. "Leena's family is noble, and she pines for the extravagant lifestyle they once had. I keep telling her that she is fortunate to be here—safe and alive."

I agreed with Miss Belmont but bit my tongue. The wealthy and nobility of Russia had been stripped of their wealth, property, status, and in some cases...their lives. Many fled Russia to safety in Europe and other countries. Everyone knew of the sad fate of the tsar and his family. Others whispered it had been preventable, if they had only moved with the twentieth century and given the ordinary people some hand in governing their lives.

"We may be far from Russia and Europe, but you can still find things of beauty here. I am sure the dress you selected will be quite stunning once the additional work is completed." That was as close as I could come to pointing out that my designs were just as good as anything from her home country.

Leena narrowed her dark gaze at me. "We make many sacrifices for the little lives we have here now. There are no palaces or grand balls."

I glanced at Miss Belmont, who nudged her friend with her elbow. "At least you are alive, Leena. And your family smuggled much of your wealth out of Russia. Or would you rather have been a beautifully dressed corpse after the revolutionaries executed you?"

"If your king had supported his royal cousins and given refuge to the tsar, we might have been able to return to our homeland," Miss Novikoff grumbled.

Rumours had swirled that King George had an opportunity to send a ship to collect the Russian royal family and give them a home in England. For whatever reason, no rescue was ever offered. Personally, I thought it would have taken quite a lot to soothe the troubles in Russia sufficiently to allow Miss Novikoff to return to her former life.

A soldier brushed past me and approached Miss Belmont. Her face broke into a smile and she held out her hands to the man. "There you are, my handsome soldier."

With his back to me, he placed a quick kiss on her cheek. Then he tucked her hand into the crook of his elbow and stood close to her. The peak of his cap shadowed his face, but there was something familiar about the angle of his jaw.

"Mrs D, this very special man here is Sidney. Or I should say, Lieutenant Sidney Dalton. Sidney, this is Mrs Devine, the most amazing dressmaker in all of Wellington," Miss Belmont said.

A spark exploded in my brain on hearing his name. The brother of the dead man. No wonder his features were familiar, and that also explained Miss Belmont's presence at the funeral. He must have been the pall-bearer she stared at in the photograph.

"Lieutenant Dalton," my tongue stumbled over the name as my brain scurried around trying to think what to say. "I am terribly sorry about your brother."

"Mrs Devine? You are the woman who was standing right next to Adam when he...stepped into the road." He ground his jaw and glanced away.

I clutched my handbag tighter. The family must have been told my name. Guilt already simmered inside me. The brother's reaction threw fertiliser upon it and it surged upward like Jack's beanstalk.

"Gosh, Mrs D! I didn't realise it was you who had been with Adam. How horrid." Miss Belmont's fingers tightened on the fabric of her companion's sleeve.

"I couldn't stop him," I whispered from a dry throat. "He stepped backwards straight into the path of the tram."

"Too many good men die when others do nothing. We should hold people accountable for their cowardly actions," the lieutenant spat out.

My heart stuttered and my mouth snapped shut. Cowardly? It had happened so fast. I tried. My hands curled into fists as I imagined grabbing hold of Mr Dalton's sleeve, or satchel, or *anything* to halt his backward movement.

"Do not blame her, my friend. Death comes to us all. To some sooner than others when they rush towards it," another voice with a heavy accent came from behind me.

"Yes. It was a terrible accident and there was nothing anyone could have done." Miss Belmont hugged the lieutenant's arm tight and shot me an apologetic look.

Lieutenant Dalton huffed and angled his body away from me.

"Ah. You finally roused yourself from bed to join us." Miss Novikoff narrowed her gaze at the newcomer.

"No. I was on my way home from last night when I heard all the noise. I am hungry. You said there would be breakfast." The crowd parted to allow a tall and dark man to join us. He wore a dishevelled suit, as though he had slept in it. He stood beside Miss Novikoff and from his accent and similar build, I assumed him to be related to her.

"That is Mr Boris Novikoff. Leena's brother," Miss Belmont murmured. Apparently, nobles from Russia didn't introduce one another to the hired workers who clothed them.

"It was lovely to meet you all. I shall leave you to your breakfast." My attention lingered on the Russian siblings. They were arresting to look upon, both with a heady charisma that raised the hair on the back of my neck. It was like reaching your hand out to touch a beautiful flower whose petals concealed a deadly poison.

Chapter Eight

I LEFT the group with an odd feeling of disquiet swirling through me. How unfair of Lieutenant Dalton to blame me for his brother's death, and then demand I be held accountable! Pushing aside my indignation, I focused on finding my son among the hundreds of people. As I set off in another direction, a familiar voice called my name.

"Mrs Devine!"

I glanced around as Etty pushed her way through the crowd towards me. In her wake, with the same flare of auburn hair and pointed chin as his sister trailed her brother, Patrick. Etty was smartly dressed in a deep green suit with white trim that perfectly suited her colouring. Patrick inhabited a suit that appeared to be doused with itching powder, judging by the way he tugged at his tie and kept scratching at his arms.

"Hello, Etty. Have you seen Theo and my cousin Joseph at all?" I stood on tiptoes, wondering how on earth I missed my much taller relatives. Frank and Joseph were about the same height, yet they disappeared in the sea of people. I assumed they must both be kneeling or bending over to talk to someone.

"Yes. Miss Kostas sent me to find you. They are all over there." Etty gestured further ahead of us to where the streets intersected, close to where I had left Dad and Mrs Kostas on the corner.

Patrick flushed as he shuffled from foot to foot before me. We had an inauspicious meeting in a darkened alley, where a gang he foolishly joined tried to beat up my friends and me. Since that night, he had avoided me whenever he lingered in Plimmer Steps to escort Etty home when we worked after dark.

The lad swallowed several times and glanced at his sister. "Mrs Devine, I want you to know I'm terribly sorry for what happened. I was an idiot to follow Dwyer so blindly. As Etty keeps telling me. Thank you for not taking it out on her and sacking her."

"Perhaps next time you will think how your actions might affect your family and those you care about." Etty's brother needed to pull his head out of the sand and take a hard look at the road he was walking. Not that I'd ever fire Etty because of his stupidity. I'd no more want to lose my second in command than I would hack off my right hand.

The blush crept up from under his collar and his cheeks turned bright red as though he had run a considerable distance. Patrick's Adam's apple bobbed up and down and he shuffled from foot to foot. It seemed the younger man was genuinely sorry for his foolish behaviour, and I didn't have all day to let him ponder the wrong turns he took.

"Etty is a wonderful seamstress and a most capable manager of my office. I would be lost without her, and I believe her hard work will be rewarded as we grow. I am glad to hear that you now realise how unwise it was to idolise a violent and unpredictable man," I said in a gentle tone.

Patrick slid his cap off his head and scrunched it in his hands. "I thought Geoff was a good bloke who knew about the world. Turns out I was wrong."

I patted Patrick's arm. The lad had been tormented enough, and there was no need for me to add to his discomfort. "There are still many decent blokes in this world, if you are looking for one to model yourself upon."

Etty swallowed a smile. We had both been trying to steer Patrick towards better men, but he was digging his toes in, due to those more worthy models working to enforce the laws of the land.

"Let's find everyone else, and then get ourselves a cup of tea." Etty prodded her brother to head off first and then she fell into step beside me.

We walked to the bottom of Boulcott Street where my family gathered, and an excited Theo ran up to me.

"Did you see how tall I was? And everyone cheered when I went past!" He grinned and one small hand went to his father's service medal pinned to his chest.

I patted his dark hair, and my heart swelled with

love and pride for my child. "I saw you and thought you looked marvellous. As did your Uncles Joseph and Frank. Speaking of Frank, where is he?" Scanning the surrounding faces, I couldn't spot the tall and slim man with the eerie amber eyes.

"He said he had some *associate* he needed to talk to, and that he might be along later." Joseph's brows pulled together when he said the word associate. His policeman brain appeared to have already jumped to a conclusion that meant Frank was up to something illegal or, at the very least, ill-advised.

I tried not to show my disappointment. I had been ever so slightly avoiding Frank of late. But Theo adored his uncle and their time together. With Frank's eerie similarity to his older brother, being with his uncle was the closest Theo could get to being with his deceased father. "Well, if he says he'll join us later, then I'm sure he will."

At that moment, Etty coughed into her hand. When I glanced her way, she rolled her eyes sideways to her brother and then inclined her head ever so slightly at Joseph. Ah! I nearly forgot the secret mission we plotted for today. Perhaps it was just as well Frank was absent from the renewed attempt to get Patrick talking to Joseph. It would be just our luck the impressionable lad would latch onto Frank instead and end up running some black-market operation from the back of a lorry.

I grabbed hold of Joseph's arm before my relative

tried to escape. "Patrick, do you remember my cousin, Joseph Sullivan?"

"We've met," Etty's brother muttered. He didn't seem openly hostile, so the army uniform instead of the constabulary blue was working to confuse him. His gaze wandered to the medals pinned on Joseph's jacket. In an instance, the young man's demeanour changed. His eyes widened, and he peered closer. A fingertip hovered by one particular medal. "You have a Military Medal!"

"Yes," Joseph measured out the single word, as though reluctant to elaborate.

"Blimey. How did you get it?" A keen interest lit Patrick's hazel gaze, and it appeared we had finally pulled him over the hump of resistance about Joseph being a constable. All it took was a medal awarded for an act of gallantry and devotion to duty while under fire. None of us knew the full story behind what exactly Joseph did that earned such recognition. In typical Kiwi fashion, he downplayed it.

Joseph shrugged, but I caught the way he darted a look to Etty. "I was just helping my mates, like anyone would do."

After a brief consultation, it was decided that we would head up to the Shepherd's Arms. Dad was keen to chat with his mates and the pub would be laying on a breakfast spread following the dawn service. Theo would be allowed to attend, as many children would be among the crowd.

"I could murder a cup of tea," Mrs Kostas said as she linked arms with Sam.

"Etty, I hope you and Patrick will join us?" Then, before my assistant could answer, I tugged on Joseph's sleeve. "If you have your motorcycle parked somewhere nearby, could you please give Etty a ride up the hill? She hurt her foot when she dropped a bolt of fabric on it, and I don't like the idea of her walking too far."

Etty opened her mouth to protest she'd done no such thing, then she snapped it shut again when Joseph cast her a shy smile.

"Of course," he murmured. "I left it down here earlier."

My assistant bestowed a charming smile on the tall constable. "Thank you, Mr Sullivan, that would be most kind of you."

A sweet blush swept over Joseph's face at being addressed by the petite Etty. "You can call me Joseph, Miss Doyle."

"Only if you will call me Etty," my assistant replied as Joseph gestured to where his motorcycle was parked just a bit further along the road.

With a sense of satisfaction, I watched Joseph offer his arm to Etty for the short walk, and then he steadied her as she climbed onto the back of the Triumph. Having seen the seed planted between those two made another idea sprout in my head. "Has anyone seen George King this morning?"

"I saw him talking to a couple of chaps while we were looking for Joseph and Theo," Sam said.

"Where?" I blamed the memories stirred up by Anzac Day. My mothering instinct seemed to demand I ensure everyone I considered part of my wider family was cared for today. I had to lay eyes on the troubled man. He too had served, and it was entirely possible that what George had experienced at war had contributed to why he built his own world to inhabit.

"Over there. Why?" Sam pointed to one side of the building across the road and to where a stand of trees was holding out against the expansion of the city.

"I need to find George and check that he will have breakfast, then I'll join you at the Arms. Can you keep an eye on everyone?"

Sam gave me a salute and a wink.

I struck off in the direction my friend indicated to find the man who thought himself the child of King George. He might not be an actual prince, but I considered our George a prince among men. Even though he had nothing, he would give the shirt off his back to another. That made me ponder how often it was those with nothing whose hearts held the greatest kindness. Yet those with unimaginable wealth were cold and indifferent to their fellow man. Perhaps true wealth should be measured by a person's actions and not coins.

I found George in the building's shadow. An old jacket around his too-thin shoulders and a troubled look on his face as he stared off into the dispersing soldiers and families. He hadn't marched with the other soldiers, even though he deserved to stand among them. George had served and done his bit to secure freedom for us all. The others shouldn't shun him if the experience damaged his mind instead of his body.

"Hello, George. Is everything all right?" There was no trace of the mysterious men who Sam saw talking to him. No one else stood within a ten-foot radius of him, as though they feared venturing too close and catching his delusion of grandeur.

"Mrs Devine!" He turned and beamed at me, the smile transforming his face. "Nature has provided a glorious autumn day to honour our fallen."

"Yes." While cold, the sky above didn't contain a single cloud and even the constant wind behaved. I rubbed the ring on my left hand. Odd how even the vaguest mention of Freddie made it itch against my skin. "Will you be catching up with your old comrades?"

His wide smile diminished a little. "I don't think any of them want a pint with old Mad George. Besides, I enlisted when I was living in Auckland, and those lads don't venture past the Bombay Hills."

"I understand most Aucklanders think that New Zealand ends there, and they would fall off the edge of the world if they tried to traverse the hills." A gentle rivalry existed between Auckland and the rest of New Zealand. Those who lived in the city up north deemed anything south of them (marked by the range known as the Bombay Hills) not worthy of their attention for being too *provincial*. That led to me wondering why Miss Novikoff and her family didn't move north. She might find others up there who shared her disdain for our countrified ways.

George barked in laughter. "Yet somehow Meg and I can ride back and forth over the Bombays without disappearing off the face of this earth."

It reassured me to see the gentle humour in his blue eyes. "That is because you love this land and it will always look after you. I hope you have a good day, George. I wanted to find you to say hello and to make sure you get a hearty breakfast into you."

He took my hand and bent over it in a courtly manner. "I can assure you, my dear Mrs Devine, that I shall partake of a fine repast this morning. As laid on by the wonderful ladies here today."

Letting me go, he gestured to the stalls set up on the edges of the lawn around Parliament. Covered with crisp white tablecloths, the tables held a variety of covered plates and trays. The women had baked up a storm to ensure that every soldier would have something warm in their stomach today. They even had little camp stoves to keep the tea, coffee, and sausages hot.

"I'll not get between you and a well-deserved cup of tea. I hope I'll see you during the week in a quieter moment." Waving, I set off up the road to catch up with my family.

The sun was hovering above the horizon when I pushed into the warmth and light of the Shepherd's Arms. My family was seated at what we considered our table in the far corner. Theo knelt on a chair to have a better view of the tightly packed crowd. Probably trying to spot any of his school chums. Joseph was chatting to Etty and appeared to be relaxing around the fiery Irishwoman. Or at the very least, he wasn't blushing and stuttering. Her brother sat on the other side and hung on every word, so I assumed they had somehow managed to get Joseph to talk about something war-related. I crossed paths with Sam as she returned from the bar carrying our tea and coffee.

On seeing me, she thrust the tray into my hands. "You take care of hot drinks for that lot, and I'll fetch some plates of food."

Balancing the full and heavy tray with care, I slid it onto the table. It held a coffee pot, a teapot, a milk jug, and a hot cocoa for Theo. Empty mugs were waiting in the middle of the table, along with the sugar pot. Mrs Kostas poured and handed around drinks and conversation flowed. Sam returned with a tray carrying scones and bacon butties. Theo grinned at the treat of a bacon sandwich for breakfast, and the small boy was soon munching away.

I selected a scone. As tempting as the butties were, part of me didn't want bacon fat on my fingers. Watching Theo wipe his hands on his sleeve made me shudder. There were times that no matter how hard you tried, manners refused to stick in small boys. Or larger ones, I thought, as I observed Dad licking a dribble of bacon grease from the side of his hand.

Chapter Nine

After we had cleared the plates of scones and bacon butties, Patrick excused himself and beelined for a group at one end of the bar. Etty rolled her eyes and blew out a snort.

"Where has he gone?" I asked as I finished my tea and studied the men who had lured Patrick away from our table.

"That's Da and his mate, Mr Griffin. The other two lads who look about the same age as Patrick are Mr Griffin's sons. No doubt they'll all be talking about events back home," Etty said.

Hearing it was the group of men that Adam Dalton was possibly tied up with perked my interest. The older men were leading the conversation, not surprising given that Mr Griffin had escaped the violent uprising with his family only a few years ago. Etty's family had immigrated to New Zealand when she was only a small child and Patrick was a babe.

"Do your parents regret their decision to come here?" What a difficult choice to have made. To leave everyone and everything behind that you know and love. To put your young family on a crowded, dark, and damp ship for weeks, only to land in a country where you knew no one. At least there were several similarities between New Zealand and Ireland. Neither of our countries had snakes. Thinking of the slithering reptiles made a shudder work down my spine.

Etty pushed a stray auburn curl back behind her ear. "I don't think so, not really. Da likes to make out that he's missing out on being in the action and fighting for Ireland against the English. But I think Ma is glad we are here, and he's not at risk of getting shot or killed."

The Irish fight for Home Rule had turned into a war for independence. Ruptures were forming in the country, and I feared that many more people would die before the issue was settled.

"War is always more appealing in stories than it is when you stand in the middle of it," Joseph said in a quiet tone.

I squeezed Joseph's arm and glanced at Etty. "We are glad you came home to us in one piece, Joseph. Although I swear war made you taller." It certainly added bulk to his frame. I wondered if the army had utilised Joseph as a packhorse, that he had sprouted all those muscles.

The ghost of a smile tugged at his lips. "It was all that time standing in muck. It acted like a fertiliser."

"I'd like to have a tall man around. There's always something on a top shelf I can't reach," Etty sighed and looked up at him through lowered lashes.

The conversation among the Irishmen appeared to be heating up, as arms were waved and their volume increased. Someone shushed them, and they cast nervous looks around the room. Then their conversation continued in hushed tones with their heads bent together. Patrick leaned in with the other two lads, to catch what was being said by their fathers.

Given my urge to learn if the group posed any threat to the prince, I had the perfect opportunity to eavesdrop. Although I doubted they would say anything revolutionary and incriminating in a packed bar. I also wanted to leave Etty gently flirting with my cousin and had hopes that Joseph might have asked her out by the time I returned.

"Who wants more coffee?" I asked, picking up the empty pot.

Without waiting for a response, I marched up to the bar, handed over the coffee pot, and asked for a refill. Then I leaned on the bar and pretended great interest in the printed menu as I waited. The snippets I overheard from the group were about how Ireland should be free of England's grip.

"You can't trust the English. They're a pack of dirty liars. They promised Ireland would be free to rule herself and then ignored the laws they had passed to make it happen." Mr Doyle slammed one fist into his palm.

Patrick nodded along with his father's words and murmurs of agreement came from the others.

"This is our chance, isn't it, Da? Our lads are fighting back home, but we can make them sit up and pay us attention," one of the other lads said.

"Too right, Donald. All the world's eyes will be upon us in just a few days." Mr Griffin patted his son on the shoulder.

As I listened, it struck me that what they discussed didn't seem to mesh with the last words of Adam Dalton. He had specifically mentioned the prince, who didn't make or implement laws. Or did they target him because he represented England, or would, once crowned as king?

"The timing has to be right. We'll only get one shot and can't afford for it to go wrong," Mr Griffin said.

That definitely sounded like some sort of plot. The words *one shot* made icy dread pour into my stomach.

"We'll be ready, don't you worry," Donald answered.

The barman handed across the full coffee pot, and I wandered back to our table. Theo became restless and couldn't sit still (no coffee required!) and darted off to find his friends.

After a pleasant couple of hours, it was time to round up the family and head home. Theo was subdued, the early start already taking its toll, and I expected him to fall asleep later in the afternoon. Which meant a quiet afternoon to tackle the hand sewing needed to finish the gown for Miss Belmont.

Monday morning dawned grey and miserable, as though having behaved for Anzac Day, Mother Nature threw all her excess horrid weather at us. Cold rain fell as I readied Theo for school, and I indulged in the dream of having an automobile to take my son on the short trip to school, so neither of us became drenched. Umbrellas were pointless in Wellington as the wind turned them inside out. Instead, Theo wore a thick woollen coat, and I squished a hat over his ears.

Then we set off, heads bent into the prevailing wind to stop the horizontal rain from stinging our eyes. As soon as we neared the gates, he took off at a gallop to join the other children inside the schoolhouse. I pitied the teachers with that many children stuck inside at lunchtime. Although knowing the boys, they would head out to poke sticks into puddles regardless of the weather.

Water leaked down the back of my neck by the time I entered the warmth and light of the atrium for my business. I took a moment to shake the excess water from myself before I walked up the stairs.

Mrs Mac sat at the reception desk with small containers of beads spread before her. She glanced up at me. "You look like a drowned rat. The kettle has not long boiled and a cup of tea should warm you up." She set aside the red silk and pushed back her chair.

"Thank you, Mrs Mac. There was an unexpected downpour between the school and any shelter offered by the buildings along Lambton Quay." I followed her into the kitchen and peeled off my outer layers. Then I hung my coat and cardigan on hooks to dry. I even toed off my wet shoes, thankful I kept a change of clothes in my locker in the atelier.

Soon I had donned a dry apron and shoes. Sitting in my warm office watching droplets run down the glass, I had a mug of tea in my hands as I reviewed the day's work.

My ladies laboured much longer hours than I liked, but it would mean we would complete every gown required for the brief royal visit. I tallied the numbers in my ledger. If all my clients paid their bills promptly (and experience taught me to no longer extend credit!) then I would have sufficient profit to pay a bonus to everyone for their hard work.

Mid-morning, I needed a break from being bent over the account books and my brain was stuffed to overflowing with numbers and calculations. Grabbing my now dry coat, I headed off to the post office to collect our parcels of embellishments that we needed for the final touches. On the way back, as I readied to cross the road, I spied George on the corner. He had his collar turned up and his chin tucked in against the cold and rain. He looked miserable, and visible shivers ran over his frame.

I walked over and tapped him on the shoulder. "Hello George, what are you doing out here in the rain?"

"Grace! I'm waiting for my entourage. They

promised to meet me here at ten-thirty." He glanced up and down the street. What pedestrians were out were all hurrying to get to their destinations as quickly as possible.

A motherly pang shot through me, even though he was older than me. I couldn't leave him like this any more than if he had been a cold and shivering puppy. "It is closer to eleven now. Perhaps the weather has detained them. Why don't we get a hot cup of tea while you wait?"

He heaved a sigh, then nodded. "I could do with warming up."

There was a little café at the end of Lambton Quay, past the cable car and opposite the corner dominated by the bank. While diminutive in size, the shop served hot tea and coffee to workers hurrying past and the owner wouldn't cast judgement on George.

Linking my arm with his, we carried on down the road. "You need a decent waterproof coat with winter on its way, George. Something to keep you warm and dry."

"I had one once, lost it somewhere up north. I always rather fancied myself in a cape." He swept out one arm in a dramatic gesture, and I could imagine an inky opera cape swirling around him.

Ideas sparked in my brain for something more practical than velvet eveningwear. There was a fabric that would be a superb outer for a cloak—sailors and farmers used waxed cotton to keep wind and water away. I could line it with a patchwork of wool made from all our winter offcuts. "Leave it to me, George. I will whip something up for you before it turns much colder."

In the café, George settled at the little table in the window, where he could watch for his entourage. I paid for a pot of tea and a meat pie to warm his belly. I offered a silent apology to Sam for not patronising the Kostas Bakery for a pie but knew my friend would understand. The fare here was not as good, but it was substantial and filling.

I sipped the strong gumboot tea and worried that people might seek to take advantage of gentle George. Sam saw him chatting with a couple of men after the Anzac Day service, and I wondered if it was the same individuals or part of the same group. "How does one acquire an entourage, George? Did you interview for the position, or is it a hereditary thing the aristocracy does?"

He grinned at me from around his meat pie and winked. He politely swallowed his mouthful first, before telling me the tale. "They approached me. Good men, all of them. They recognise the injustice of me being left to languish in New Zealand while my father ignores my existence over there in Britain."

"I am glad you have found more supporters." I wanted to believe that a good bunch of blokes who had his best interests at heart had approached George. But a twinge in my gut said there was some ulterior motive at play here. Just like when a certain boy asked to see what Theo had in his lunch box, so he could upend it on the ground. If these gentlemen were playing a trick on George, well…I would do something about it. Perhaps I could discuss their behaviour with their mothers, just like I did over the spilt lunch incident.

George finished his pie and leaned closer to me, looking around first to ensure no one eavesdropped on our conversation. "They are determined to organise a meeting with my half-brother while he is here. We just need to decide on the most appropriate venue. I thought that when his motorcar drove into Wellington, I could stand in the middle of the road."

"Oh, George, don't go doing that. What if the policemen with him don't recognise you and they run you over?" I didn't like the idea of any plan that placed George in harm's way or took advantage of his beliefs to further someone else's ends.

He scratched his chin. "The grand dinner would be more appropriate, or the ball. My men are working on securing me an invitation. Deuced odd though, isn't it, to think I have to have an invitation to an event in *my* honour."

"Sadly, not everyone recognises you as the Prince of Wales and heir apparent, George. You must be tolerant of others until such a time as you are officially confirmed by the king." I sipped my tea and glanced at my wristwatch. I should be getting back to my atelier, but needed to ensure George was going to be all right first.

"Soon, Grace, soon." He patted my arm. "Are you

sure you won't reconsider being my future queen? Events are afoot, you know."

I am sure many young girls dreamed of marrying a prince and going off to live in a palace. But my dreams had always revolved around clothing the royals, not being one. "I'm not one for living under a spotlight. But when you find a princess, I would love the opportunity to design a grand ball gown for her."

"Ha! An easy deal to make with you." Movement outside the window caught his eye, and George pushed back his chair. "Must dash, Mrs Devine. There're the chaps, now. Many thanks for the tea and pie."

"My pleasure, George." I finished my tea as I watched him hurry along the road to where two men stood. They huddled under a verandah to escape the rain that pelted nearly horizontally with the force of the wind. One man was tall and dark and dressed in a well-cut wool coat. The other, lighter skinned with brown hair. Recognition flared in my brain since I had only met them the day before.

Mr Boris Novikoff and Lieutenant Sidney Dalton. What business did those two gentlemen have with George?

George crossed the street, and soon the three of them disappeared from view along a side road. I should follow and see what they were up to. But there was also a phenomenal amount of work to do, which included finishing the gown for Miss Novikoff. If I orchestrated a reason to go and see her, perhaps I could find a way to ask how her brother knew the man who thought himself a prince.

Snippets of an overheard conversation flowed through my worried brain. An Irishman murmuring, 'The timing has to be right. We'll only get one shot...'

But neither Mr Novikoff nor the lieutenant was Irish or part of that group. Did the Dalton brothers have a closer association with those agitating for freedom in Ireland than I knew? Worries multiplied inside me as to how George King was tied up with the men. I doubted they genuinely supported his claims and most likely they saw him as a diversion.

Another phrase bubbled up in my head. One spoken by Lieutenant Dalton. *People should be held accountable for their actions.* A light bulb clicked on in my head. Those words were eerily familiar to those plucked from Adam Dalton's memory. *That royal bastard will pay for what they did. He should be held accountable.*

Lieutenant Dalton was the man who spoke in the memory! If he did anything to place George King at risk, I would ensure the lieutenant was indeed held accountable for his actions. Even if I risked losing a lovely client like Miss Belmont in the process.

I rose and tucked my parcels and bag against my chest as determination steeled my spine. I needed help, the sort that only Mrs Cooper could provide.

Chapter Ten

I HURRIED up the road to Plimmer Steps, protecting the parcels in my arms from the fierce rain. Then I dispensed the packages to sighs from my ladies as the contents spilt out to reveal beads, sequins, and delicate tiny buttons in a dizzying array of colours.

Despite the blur of activity in the workroom, I needed to relieve the itch in my head with a pencil and my sketchbook. Grabbing a clean sheet, I quickly drew the outline of a three-quarter-length cloak for George. I added deep pockets on the outside and a hood to keep the rain from trickling down the back of his neck. The garment needed enough flare to it so that when mounted on his horse, it would protect the equine's flank as well.

When I was happy with the length and drape on the page, I went through to the storeroom to see what I could find. In a back corner was a bolt of waxed cotton, left over from making a coat for Dad when he went hunting. The stiff fabric was invented for sail cloth in the late 1700s. It took many more years, and probably a keen-eyed woman, to realise it was perfect for waterproof clothing for hunters, farmers, and gamekeepers.

Next, I grabbed the basket of cabbage. Not the smelly vegetable, but the name given to the offcuts after we have taken our pattern pieces. In my storeroom, the cabbage was sorted by type. Delicate silks and chiffons together, robust wools in another basket.

Since we had recently cut out several warm winter coats, there was sufficient in the basket to make a patchwork lining. I carried the basket and bolt back through to my office. Once the cutting table was free, I would unroll the waxed canvas and cut the shapes for the outer of the cloak and the deep hood. Stitching the offcuts together for the lining would be a task to occupy my evenings.

Time drifted by like a fast-flowing river as I sketched spring and summer outfits we would make over the winter months. When my back protested the hours spent hunched over my desk, I glanced at my wristwatch and made a decision. I would risk Mrs Cooper's disapproval with an unscheduled late afternoon visit.

Leaving the capable Etty in charge for an hour or two, I left clutching a basket with fabric samples and sketches. The contents were my flimsy excuse for calling upon Mrs Cooper unannounced. I struck off for Thorndon and hoped she was home for me.

When I rapped on the glossy black door, the maid

who opened it stared at me blankly, even though I was a regular visitor, and she knew my name.

"Is Mrs Cooper available, please? I have important issues pertaining to the royal visit to discuss with her, and it simply cannot wait until our usual Sunday afternoon tea." I waved my basket, but the word *royal* was all I needed to say to galvanise her into action.

The maid's eyes widened, and she stared at my basket as though I had shrunk the prince and had him stashed away among the fabric. "I shall go and ask her, Mrs Devine."

At least I was allowed inside to wait and wasn't left to huddle against the side of the house to protect me from the blustery wind rolling off the harbour.

A few minutes later, the maid reappeared. "She will see you, Mrs Devine. This way."

She led me down the hall and into the library. Mrs Cooper sat in a leather armchair with wide rolled arms set before the fire. A book rested in her lap. She looked at ease, but then anyone would have been surrounded by so many books and with a cosy fire to chase away any chill.

She arched one finely plucked eyebrow. "Grace. What an unexpected intrusion. I understand it concerns all that fuss and nonsense surrounding Edward?"

Gosh. She called the prince...*Edward*. I didn't know that was allowed. "Yes. We have some terribly last-minute adjustments to a few gowns, and I thought to seek your opinion."

"Tea," Mrs Cooper called out to her maid and then she gestured to the armchair set at an angle to hers.

I shrugged off my coat, and the maid took it away with her. Then I sat with the basket on my knee and pulled out the fabrics. All the while telling my feeble story about wanting to ensure each of my clients had her chance to shine and that no two appeared too similar. I had sketches of ways to alter gowns that mimicked the same lines a little too closely. As we discussed ideas, the maid returned with the laden tea tray.

Mrs Cooper poured and offered an astute comment here and there as I waved my sketches. All too soon, I had reached the last scrap of silk and the last piece of paper. My shoulders sagged as I gathered everything together and wondered how to broach the subject that brought me to her door.

Fortunately, nothing escaped my mentor's sharp mind or piercing gaze. She regarded me over the rim of her tea cup. "Now that we have that out of the way, what is the real reason behind your visit?"

I opened my mouth to protest, but I had the same inability to lie to Mrs Cooper as I found in the presence of Detective Archer.

"You forget I entered society at Queen Victoria's court. Intrigue and deceit swirled thicker there than at any time during the war. You learned how to spot someone with a hidden motive. What is yours?" She stated it all so matter-of-factly, it was impossible to take offence.

I set down the teacup and clasped my hands on my

lap so that nerves didn't make me fidget. "When I witnessed Adam Dalton's dying words, he muttered a vague reference to some plot against Prince Edward. I find myself unable to leave the matter to the police. Particularly when someone is involved who might not be perceived by the constabulary as posing any threat."

The manicured eyebrows shot up, and her blue gaze widened. "Do tell. Since you have come to me, I surmise it is someone who moves in my circles. Someone well placed to sidle up next to the prince and pull a weapon from within their evening jacket."

The situation she described was exactly what bothered me. Or not so much a knife being pulled from an evening jacket, as one slid from a sheath attached by a decorative garter to a thigh. Detective Archer might look at protestors, communists, or the disenfranchised when perhaps his attention should be aimed higher among society.

"I do not wish to cause offence among my clients," I murmured. Or lose their custom. It was a fine line to nose into the affairs of the men who were close to the women I dressed. Like brothers and beaus. If I crossed that line, I might find clients cancelling. Again.

Mrs Cooper picked up the teapot and poured more of the fragrant brew into my nearly empty cup. "You know I am the soul of discretion, Grace. Everything you tell me remains strictly between us. I have found it quite invigorating helping you track down murderers. Now we shall turn our minds to anarchists and who might want to strike against the royal family."

I either trusted the older woman or had to let go of my concerns. Since the latter wasn't possible, I reminded myself of Mrs Cooper's impeccable reputation for keeping her lips sealed. "I fear it is someone who feels King George did not do enough for *their* royal family." I held the cup in two hands to warm my suddenly chilled flesh.

Mrs Cooper sucked in a breath, not needing anything more than that tidbit. "Well. That was unexpected. The Novikoffs."

"Apparently Miss Novikoff decided at the last moment that she would attend the Citizens Ball. Miss Belmont brought her along to her fitting and asked if I could find a suitable gown for her friend amongst those we had made for the showing." Had the sudden change of mind been brought about after discussions with her brother? How horrifying if the femme fatale lured the prince close, only to thrust a knife into his heart. At least the red silk wouldn't show bloodstains. But I didn't want to develop a reputation for *gowns to die for* if they kept being linked to murders.

"They are an odd family. I imagine she didn't so much as ask about a gown as made it sound like some sort of imperial demand," Mrs Cooper huffed.

I managed a weak smile. "I did rather get the impression that *no* would not be taken as an answer. Luckily, one of the completed dresses was deemed acceptable with the addition of some beading. It fit her rather well when she tried it on."

"The red silk?"

"Yes." This was why I trusted Mrs Cooper's advice. She had an impeccable fashion sense, probably bred into her family over the centuries courtesy of their noble British blood.

Mrs Cooper nodded. "I can only imagine how stunning she will be in that one. But her family seems to think they are still in Russia with the tsar running everything, and we are all serfs meant to satisfy their every need."

I hoped my curiosity about their flight across half the globe might be satisfied. "I wonder that they came so far, when they could have had a luxurious life in Europe."

"That bit is odd. Most of those who fled settled in Europe somewhere. The Novikoffs left their country before the real trouble started, and my sources tell me they managed to extract most of their wealth. They are probably the richest family in Wellington if not all of New Zealand. Perhaps they wanted to be the big fish in a very small pond. In Europe, they would always be reminded that while noble, they weren't *royal*." Mrs Cooper placed a blush pink macaroon on a delicate plate and handed it to me.

I took the treat and hoped Sam wouldn't smell macaroon on my breath. My friend refused to offer them at the Kostas Bakery. She deemed them *too fancy*, as they weren't filling enough for the working lads.

"Miss Novikoff could remedy her lack of royal status if she catches the eye of Prince Edward." I tried to imagine a Russian queen on the British throne. Some whispered that was why King George didn't rescue the royal family—Queen Mary didn't want the tsarina stealing her limelight in England. A Russian daughter-in-law who would replace her might make for awkward family dinners.

"What makes you think they harbour any ill feelings towards the Prince of Wales?" Mrs Cooper nibbled one side of her macaroon.

"I am friendly with George King, who believes he is the true heir to the throne. He told me that a couple of chaps support his claim and have a plan for him to meet his *half-brother*. Then earlier today, I saw Mr Novikoff and another gentleman with George King, and I worry about their true intentions."

"Another? Who else is part of this hypothetical conspiracy?" That keen gaze sliced through my reluctance to admit everything.

"Lieutenant Sidney Dalton, who is the beau of Miss Belmont." Two wealthy clients, both associated with men seeking to use George King. But who was the puppet master and who was the mere pawn?

Mrs Cooper wiped her fingers on a linen napkin draped over her knee. "Dalton? There is a name I haven't heard for a few years."

"Is the family in your circle?" I assumed they were swimming in the upper echelon of society, unless Miss Belmont was stepping out with the soldier to scandalise her family.

"Oh, yes. On the fringes. There was some scandal a few years ago, but I can't remember it now." She frowned and stared off into the corner of the library as she sought to gather the details.

"I believe the scandal surrounded Major Dalton. Some campaign that went terribly wrong with the needless loss of lives that resulted in his...discharge from the army." I supplied the missing information courtesy of Frank.

A long sigh blew over Mrs Cooper's lips. "Now I remember. Horrible affair, and his poor wife was quite cut out of things. Although, from what I recall, Sidney is a decent enough chap. I imagine he is being led by Boris. That one has the magnetism of Rasputin, from what I hear. Certainly, enough socialites flock to him." She set down her cup as her thoughts turned to the younger generation of wealthy Wellingtonians.

My newest client's brother had a dangerous attractiveness about him. Fabulous wealth would add to his allure. But how to get close to discover if there was any truth to my suspicions? "I'm not sure what I can do, but I need a way to talk to Miss Novikoff to determine if she is caught up in any conspiracy of her brother's. If my fears have any basis, then I will take the information to Detective Archer."

"Well, you need a much better excuse than the one that brought you here, if you want to gain admittance to their home." She chuckled to herself. After a moment's thought, she added, "Jewellery. We can say that you need to know what jewellery Leena intends to wear, in case you need to alter the neckline of the gown to accommodate the piece."

Oh. Brilliant. The Grecian inspired drape at the front might need lowering to show off a necklace. Then a particular word stuck in my head. "We?"

A conspiratorial grin spread over the older woman's face. "You don't think I'm staying here, do you? I shall telephone Mrs Novikoff and inform her that we will be visiting this evening."

It never ceased to amaze me who the other woman knew and the places where she could gain admittance. "Are you friends with Mrs Novikoff?"

"Good Lord, no. I'd call us adversaries. But I do so enjoy sparring with her. Besides, I might find out a snippet or two while you talk to her daughter. Let us hope Boris is lurking somewhere in the house." She winked and rose from her seat.

I ate the rest of my macaroon while I waited. My gaze was drawn to the neatly shelved books that formed two walls in the room. Imagine having enough time to read them all. There was my definition of wealth and luxury. To do nothing except recline on a chaise, read, and eat macaroons.

A scant fifteen minutes later, Mrs Cooper returned. "It is all arranged. I shall have my driver collect you at a quarter to eight if you would be so good as to wait on Tinakori Road. We have an appointment at eight with the Novikoffs, before they dine."

Dinner after eight? That was an hour after Theo's bedtime. I would be free, but I couldn't imagine waiting until that late at night to eat. I stared at my mentor and questions must have been written all over my face.

"What time do you usually dine, Grace?"

"Dinner is on the table at six, Mrs Cooper." That was the whole point behind six o'clock closing. Men were supposed to roll straight home and sit themselves down at the dinner table.

The older woman barked in laughter. "There is the fundamental difference between New Zealand and England and Europe. The aristocracy dines late because our entertainments don't start until after dark. Nor do we have to rise before noon. We don't have cows waiting to be milked at dawn."

Or children who woke with the sparrows and expected breakfast. The upper classes lived an entirely different sort of life, and I observed it with the same fascination as when I stared at the tiger at the zoo. "I shall be ready and waiting outside the Shepherd's Arms."

With our battle plan made, I took my leave to ponder how, exactly, I was going to steer the forthcoming conversation to learn more from the Novikoffs. Or perhaps I would play the role I was more suited for, that of a seamstress. Mrs Cooper was eminently more suited to spying, and I would gladly hand that portion of the evening over to her.

Chapter Eleven

On the dot of seven forty-five, a long and sleek motor vehicle slowed to a stop beside me as I waited in the light thrown through the windows of the pub. The driver hurried from his side to open the door for me. Murmuring my thank you, I slid onto the leather seat beside Mrs Cooper.

"Whereabouts do the Novikoff family live?" I asked as the driver got back into his seat and the vehicle moved off so gently, I wouldn't have spilt a drink if I had been holding one.

"They live in the big brick house perched above Oriental Bay, so they can survey everyone below." Mrs Cooper huddled into her wool coat. A chill pervaded the interior of the motorcar.

"Gosh." I knew the place. So large and imposing that, from the street level, it was often mistaken for a private school or a nunnery. "I bet that feels the full brunt of the southerly when winter arrives."

Mrs Cooper laughed. "I don't think a Wellington chill compares to winter in St Petersburg where the snow lies several feet deep."

Her driver expertly navigated Wellington's roads and wound up the hill towards the house with its spectacular views of the harbour. I let myself out while the driver held the door open for his employer.

Mrs Cooper charged along the path and rapped on the door. I trailed behind and wondered what we would find inside.

A maid answered, glanced at Mrs Cooper and immediately stood to one side to admit us. Whatever the combative nature of the relationship between Mrs Cooper and Mrs Novikoff, the maid knew well enough not to leave the matron waiting on the doorstep.

A subdued air hung over the rambling house. I stood with my feet contained within one square tile and took in the surroundings. The entranceway had a patterned tile around the edge, with curling vines on a muted yellow with a deep red edge. In the centre, a larger image of the spreading vine reached out over several tiles. The dark panelled walls were softly lit by widely spaced lights. A staircase curved up one side of the entranceway to a landing illuminated by a stained-glass window. Rich burgundy rugs covered the floor. As I stood staring down a hall, I felt like an adventurer holding aloft a torch about to venture into a cave. Part of me wanted to run off and explore, certain the house was a museum containing rare and wonderful treasures.

But I didn't. I took my cues from Mrs Cooper and tried very hard to feign disinterest in my lush surroundings.

A petite older woman appeared in a doorway and approached. Dressed in a gorgeous blue velvet gown covered in silver embroidery with a train that brushed the floor, it would have been the height of fashion in the era before the war. She had the same dark colouring as the younger Novikoffs and an imperial way of carrying herself, such that I had to stop myself from dipping at the knees in a curtsey.

"Temperance," Mrs Novikoff said in a cool tone.

"Tatiana." Mrs Cooper returned the opening salvo of painful politeness, stripped off her gloves and coat, and handed them to the maid.

I likewise removed my coat but kept hold of my satchel containing my sketch pad, pencils, and a tape measure. The two formidable women stared at each other long enough that I clutched my bag tighter in case I needed to use it as a shield if one of them suddenly produced a weapon.

"Leena is in the red drawing room. I trust this intrusion won't last long. We are entertaining this evening." Mrs Novikoff gestured across the expansive tiled entranceway to a set of double doors.

"I wouldn't dream of staying long in this chilly house. Why, Mrs Devine and I will hardly have time to finish the drinks you will offer us." Mrs Cooper swept past the shorter woman and into the room.

Miss Novikoff sat on a sofa, staring into the fire. A polished wooden phonograph against one wall played a record. The faint strains of music curled around the room. I dreamed of having my own phonograph to play whatever I wanted to listen to whenever I wanted. Dad and I made do with the radio and the musical whims of the hosts.

Mr Novikoff sat at a small table behind the long sofa. He appeared to be repairing a radio. The back of the device sat to one side and the inner workings were exposed. Mr Novikoff tinkered with wires inside it. A pair of pliers in one hand as he squinted at the mechanism.

"Good evening, Miss Novikoff. Thank you for seeing me." A tense atmosphere built in the room somewhat akin to being sent to the principal's office at school for bad behaviour. Would Mrs Novikoff whip out a cane and rap me over the knuckles if I did something wrong?

"Let us get this over with. I can hear Boris's stomach rumbling from here." Miss Novikoff slid from the chaise and sat before a low table that held a squat leather box.

"I am a man of vast appetites!" Mr Novikoff waved the pliers, then with his other hand he grabbed a red wire and peered at the copper visible at the end.

The box before my client looked like a small piece of luggage, with a hinged side and a battered appearance. A leather strap could be buckled to hold it shut.

Miss Novikoff undid the strap and unlatched the front. She swung it to one side, like a miniature door. This revealed a series of drawers. Now it really did remind me of travelling luggage that functioned like furniture.

When she pulled open one drawer, I gasped. Resting on black velvet was a glittering necklace of diamonds. Each gem was the size of a fingernail.

"Diamonds or rubies?" Miss Novikoff asked no one in particular.

"Rubies, of course," Mrs Cooper answered.

The Russian woman closed one drawer and opened another, while I wondered if it would be rude to ask her to open every single one so my eyes could feast on the incredible collection. Never again would I see such magnificent jewels. Mrs Cooper had been right when she said the family escaped Russia with much of their wealth. Staring at the gems made a sad story flit through my mind. Rumours whispered that the Romanov women had sewn the family jewels into their corsets. When the order came to execute them, they didn't die as the bullets couldn't penetrate their glittering armour. The soldiers were forced to bayonet the unfortunate women to death.

A shudder worked down my spine as I wondered at the truth of the tale and how jewellery of such beauty could result in such a horrid end.

Miss Novikoff lifted a necklace from its soft bed of velvet. In her hands, she held a large, oval ruby suspended from twisted vines of smaller rubies, all set in white gold.

"That is beautiful. What a shame there is no such thing as black gold." In my head, a necklace of red and black complemented the beadwork that Mrs Mac added to the edge of the gown.

"There is a collar with rubies and offset with obsidian beading. Not appropriate for the Russian court, of course, as it is too simple." Mrs Novikoff bustled forward and pulled out a drawer towards the bottom of the box. From it, she lifted a piece that took away my last breath. Rubies of equal size formed a collar. Around the edge were tiny iridescent black beads. A triangular shape dropped from the centre to hold a single large ruby surrounded by glistening black gems. The whole piece gave the effect of splashes of fire against a night sky.

They considered this too simple to wear before the tsar? "Oh, that is incredible." I pulled out my sketch pad and tape measure. "If you wear this piece, I can lower the neckline so that the central gem rests entirely against your skin."

Mrs Novikoff tied the collar around her daughter's neck, and I measured the distance from her throat to the bottom of the central ruby. Then I made a quick sketch of the design. It would look stunning with the beaded edge to the gown that Mrs Mac laboured upon.

"Miss Novikoff will surely attract the eye of the prince," Mrs Cooper murmured as the young woman touched the rubies at her throat.

Mr Novikoff snorted. "Who cares for the English prince? Leena should be attracting the attention of our

Russian prince. But where is he, huh? In some cold, unmarked grave."

I glanced at Mrs Cooper. In such an instance, I preferred to defer to my mentor to answer questions about the ultimate resting place of the murdered Russian royal family.

Miss Novikoff undid the necklace, and the gems draped over her palm as she pulled open another drawer. "If he had lived, Tsarevich Alexei would still only be a child of fifteen. I have no interest in children."

"You could have moulded him to be whatever you wanted, and we would have been the power in Russia. Instead, our lives were stolen from us. Britain could have saved them all and supported the tsar while he suppressed the revolution," Mr Novikoff spat out the words as he tossed the pliers to the table and rose to pace the grand parlour. His hand curled into a fist as he no doubt imagined Tsar Nicholas crushing the uprising.

"Do you really think the revolution would have been brought under control so easily?" Mrs Cooper asked.

The Russian man met Mrs Cooper's steel-blue gaze. "If England had co-operated instead of turning her back, yes. Your king does not understand what we lost. Perhaps one day the fates will teach him that lesson."

The vehemence of his words startled me. This was a man who had convinced George he was part of his entourage. But I doubted Mr Novikoff would bow to anyone. What nefarious plan did he have in mind that involved my friend?

"Enough, Boris," Mrs Novikoff snapped and stared at her son until he fell silent. Then she turned to Mrs Cooper. "Are we quite done here, Temperance?"

Mrs Cooper smiled, but it was a cold thing that never touched her steel-blue eyes. "I think so, Tatiana. We shall leave you to your supper. I am sure you wish privacy to toast the memory of those you left behind in Russia."

I packed away my sketchbook and pencil and took one last wistful look at the jewellery. What would it be like to feel the weight of such gems against your skin? Were they cold, or did they warm up from the contact?

Feeling rather like Theo when he was ordered away from the toy section in the department store, I reluctantly followed Mrs Cooper back out to the motor vehicle.

"Well, that was interesting. Boris seems rather hot under the collar about King George failing to rescue the tsar," she said as we settled on the back seat.

"Yes. The question is, would he do anything to bring about a lesson in grief for the king?" I stared at the winking lights of the house as the motorcar pulled away. How far would he go to avenge the dead ruler?

Tuesday evening, I sat at the kitchen table and waited for Frank. Theo belted out 'God Save the King' at an uncomfortable pitch while Dad and I listened with rapt attention. My son was part of the school children's display for the prince, and Theo practised the song they would all sing. I wondered if the song should be renamed 'God Save the Prince's Hearing'.

The door swung open to admit Frank, who immediately slid his hat off, clasped it to his chest, and stood to attention as Theo sang the last verse.

We clapped for the performance. Rising from my chair, I kissed my son's cheek. "Well done, Theo. I am sure that Prince Edward will be most impressed by the performance from Thorndon School next week. Have a good evening with Poppa, and I will see you in the morning."

"Ready to trip the light fantastic, Gracie?" Frank held my coat open, and I slipped my arms into the sleeves.

A bubble of excitement welled up inside me. We hadn't been dancing since the night at the Cricket, which had ended with a brawl in a dark alley. I had quite forgotten about Frank until he ran out into the alley as we were leaving, worry etched deep on his face at all the commotion and sounding of the police whistles. Part of me had thought he'd run in case it was a raid. But then Frank's ties to family were strong and overrode his instinct to dodge the authorities.

"Yes. And I promise not to wander into dark alleys this time." I tried to make light of the other occasion.

Frank's gaze narrowed. "Too right you won't."

Even Dad had his eyebrows pulled together in concern that I'd find another fight to try to break up. "Try to come home uninjured, Grace. I'm relying on Frank to look after you."

A stern look passed between Dad and the man he didn't entirely want to become a larger fixture in our lives.

"I'll always look after her, if only she'd let me." Frank popped his hat back on his head.

The conversation was turning far too serious for me. I tapped Frank on the arm. "Come on, I shall dance the night away. Or at least until ten."

"Ten?" Frank stared at me, then shifted his gaze to Dad.

Dad held up his hands. "Don't look at me. I've never set a curfew for her, and hitting the sack early was never a Sullivan trait."

Frank shook his head and clucked his tongue at me. "Devines are night owls. Maybe she needs to spend more time with me for it to rub off, since Freddie wasn't around much."

"Or perhaps I inherited the trait from my mother. I wouldn't know." My words came out sharper than I intended. Both men fell silent.

"Have a lovely evening, you two," Dad said with a weak smile on his face.

Bless him. He was trying to like Frank, but I feared the actions of one brother would forever tarnish the other in Dad's eyes.

"Will do, Mr Sullivan." Frank touched his forehead in a loose salute and held the door for me.

"Good night, Dad." Grateful for the ceasefire, I took Frank's arm and headed out into the cool night.

Frank took us to The Cricket and even though it was quiet on a Tuesday evening, it suited me. After Theo's rousing performance, I wanted something quieter. The band played, and the singer crooned a blues number that eased my troubled mind. Frank ordered two drinks for us, and I tapped my foot at the bar, humming along to the music as we waited.

Then he carried the drinks to a small round table at the edge of the dance floor. I shrugged out of my coat and hung it over the back of my chair.

"What are you stewing about, Gracie? You've been awfully quiet," Frank said once we were seated.

I played with the straw in my shandy, trying to poke bubbles from the lemonade. "I worry the children will deafen the prince next week."

He huffed in laughter. "Theo does have great lungs on him. I can't imagine what a thousand kids all belting out 'God Save the King' at the same time will sound like."

"I suspect it won't matter where in Wellington you are. You will hear it." I shouldn't make fun of the children. They were all terribly excited to have their chance to perform for the royal visitor. It was a once-in-a-lifetime opportunity.

Frank sipped his beer, his amber eyes almost the

same shade as his drink. "I think it's more than Theo's singing that is bothering you. Are you not excited about your chance to glimpse the handsome prince? Many a woman hopes to catch his eye and be whisked off to London."

Admittedly, the butterflies of excitement were hatching in my stomach. But the dogs of worry were snapping at them as soon as they emerged from their cocoons. "I worry that something will happen to mar his visit."

"Dalton is dead. He's not a threat anymore." Frank took my hand.

"But what of the group he was involved in? The Irish lads are planning something." I was certain they intended to *take their shot* at the prince. "Then there are Lieutenant Dalton and Mr Boris Novikoff. They are hatching some plan with George King."

Frank let go of my hand and leaned back in his chair. "Well, whatever they planned, it's stymied now."

"What do you mean?" I took a sip through the straw.

"The police arrested George today. Apparently, it was quite a display as they bundled him into a vehicle. Took four officers to load him in the back as he shouted that he would have them all beheaded when he's king." He shook his head as he narrated what happened to the defenceless man.

"That's outrageous! George wouldn't hurt a soul." I would have words to Joseph when I got home. They couldn't arrest George just because his mind was troubled.

"I suspect the order came from higher up, to clean our streets of anybody who might cause embarrassment during the tour."

The band changed to a faster tune and Frank took hold of my hand again to pull me to my feet. I kept up my questions as he whirled me around the dance floor.

"I still wonder why Adam Dalton was involved with the Irish lads. Do you know if his brother is likewise friends with them?"

Frank shrugged. "I'll find out for you. I know where those boys drink."

"Perhaps both Dalton brothers were involved in agitating for the Irish freedom movement. Although Miss Belmont isn't Irish, from what I recollect." It might have been as simple as one brother supporting the other. That might explain why the lieutenant and Mr Novikoff were chummy with George. But why continue with the plot after Adam Dalton died? "Do you know much about Lieutenant Dalton?"

"Only what whispers went through the trenches. He should have made captain, but his father's actions tainted his reputation. The brass didn't want another stuff up, so they passed him over. I don't hear much about him these days, but then we run in different circles."

I let out a sigh. "I don't understand men or why you do things."

"A man will do all sorts of crazy things for the woman he loves." Frank's eyes simmered with an intensity that made me look away. Part of me wanted to believe he referred to something one of the Dalton brothers would do for love. Or was he referring to me?

Chapter Twelve

The newspapers overflowed with articles and photographs of the prince. Excited royalists could follow his progress through New Zealand, thanks to the detailed itinerary they published. Pins were moved along maps as the convoy travelled south. He was expected to arrive in Wellington on the third of May and would be in our city for three days.

Theo's part in the children's exhibition would take place on the lawn of Parliament. Although I suspect he was more excited about a day off from school, even though he had only started recently.

For my business, the end was in sight of the long hours and enormous workload. But we weren't quite there yet. Wednesday morning flew past in a blur of thread and fabric. Midday, I needed to clear my head and think. I left my ladies chatting and laughing in the kitchen and decided to head outside.

"I'll not be long. I just need the wind to clear away

some cobwebs," I said to Etty as I donned my coat and grabbed my bag.

My favourite place was a seat by the harbour where the good salty breeze would lift away the leaf litter in my mind.

Across Lambton Quay, I headed in as direct a line as possible for the water. I had a favourite spot, with a little jetty and old weathered seats for people to take in the view. It was quiet enough to drop a line over the side if you were so inclined to try to catch something. With a stiff breeze blowing, I expected to find the place deserted, but one man sat on the bench and stared out at sea.

Oh, well. I could ignore one person. But then something about the width of his shoulders made me look twice.

"Detective Archer." My feet stopped halfway between him and the rail. I glanced out at the wind-whipped harbour, my heart tugging me closer. My soul needed to stand with my toes over the edge of the planks so I could imagine walking on the water.

"Mrs Devine." He touched the brim of his fedora with one hand. In the other, he clutched a thick sandwich resting on brown paper.

"I came out for some fresh air and promise I'll not interrupt your lunch with angry words today." I offered an apologetic smile. The last time I encountered him here, I had hurled the accusation that he sought to ruin my business with his investigation.

A smile flitted behind his dark eyes, and he nodded.

Pleasantries out of the way, I continued on my way to the edge of the jetty and leaned my hands on the railing. The wood had been worn smooth by the many hands that clutched it over the years. Closing my eyes, I breathed in the salty breeze and let it pepper my skin.

Thoughts swirled through my mind, tossed this way and that with the whim of the wind. A dying man whose last memory was of the prince being held accountable for unknown actions and of New Zealand shaking off the British yoke. An Irishman passionate about freedom in Ireland, even though he was thousands of miles from his home. A Russian family who lost their way of life, and a son who blamed King George for not saving the tsar and his family. Then there was George King. A harmless man who I was sure was being used by others.

Or he was until he was dragged off the street as a nuisance. I caught myself before I turned and berated the detective for doing such a horrid thing. Only moments earlier, I had promised I would let him eat his lunch in peace.

Did any of the groups pose a threat to the prince? The words of Mr Griffin rattled around in my brain. They only had one shot.

My thoughts scattered as though a flock of seagulls dived through the middle of them. I couldn't concentrate, and there seemed to be an itch right between my shoulder blades. Half-turning, I glanced behind me to find the detective had tucked away his lunch and was staring at me.

He rose and joined me at the railing. "Forgive my intrusion, but you seem troubled."

I blew out a sigh and watched a foamy peak dash itself against the rock lining the harbour edge. "I come here to think. The movement of the water sorts through my problems, and sometimes, it magically tosses up the right path for me to take."

"I've been told I am a good listener and not just for confessions, if you would share with me." He leaned his forearms on the railing and watched a small yacht surge up and down with the waves.

Whether consciously or not, he took the eastern side of me, where the prevailing wind came from. His solid presence offered a calm spot in his shadow. My thoughts settled, but still, something held onto my tongue. Logic tapped me on the side of the head and said if there was *one* person to talk to about my concerns, it was Detective Archer. Then I could ease into what he did to George and demand my friend's release.

"I understand that you have little reason to trust me..."

"No. That's not the case at all." My brain leapt to his defence, even as my emotions wanted more time to consider my response. "You saved my friends, and me, that night in the alley. And you are a kind enough person to feed a hamster, left alone in a murdered man's bedroom. It is just that you will probably think me silly."

"I don't think that at all," he spoke in a soft

murmur, but his words were electricity through my body.

"Everyone is so excited about the royal visit and yet, I...I have a growing sense of dread." The more I learned, the more the dread filtered into every part of me. It wasn't supposed to work like this. I thought I would poke into a few corners, ask a few questions, and the itch would leave me alone.

He angled his body more as the wind increased in ferocity. "Because of Adam Dalton's last words, it is a reasonable concern. A royal personage is an obvious target for many disgruntled groups."

Of the groups worrying me, I picked the one closest to me personally. One who was no longer on the streets, even though his patient old mare remained at the stables in Thorndon. "Was it really necessary to arrest George King? What trumped-up charge did you use to bundle him off to a cell?"

Detective Archer laced his hands together, and he stared at his neatly clipped and buffed nails. "He has not been arrested, nor is he in a cell."

"Oh." That stalled my brain. Had Frank been wrong? No, Frank was rarely wrong with his sources of information. "Then what have you done with him?"

He took his time answering, as though he picked his way through a land-mine-strewn field. "It was considered that Mr King's continued presence on the streets at this time could constitute a threat."

Oh, honestly. "A threat to whom? George is a lovely man, and he harms no one by inhabiting his delusion. He even promised to make me his queen, but I had to politely decline. Does that make me an accessory in some way?"

The imposing man next to me swallowed a chuckle and he coughed to cover it up. "I happen to agree with you. Not about you being an accessory, but that by himself he is no threat. Unfortunately, due to his beliefs, he is prone to manipulation and could be used by others. Think of his temporary removal from the streets as for the protection of the royal personage—both of them."

I huffed and had to admit he was right. George had confided in me that his *entourage* was prepared to push his claim to the throne, and they were planning a meeting between him and the prince. It was probably for the better that he was out of their reach until after the royal visit. "Where is he, please? I'd like to know he is unharmed."

"He is at a care facility outside of Wellington. He is being well looked after and will be released once the royal visit has concluded."

Oh, George. The detective referred to a particular institution for those who were considered *not quite right upstairs* and who needed to be removed from polite society. At least from what I had seen from the road the time we had driven past, it had a big garden and a view. Unlike a prison cell. "Is he allowed visitors? He will be worried about his horse." I could ask Sam for a basket to take to George. He was fond of a warm scone with butter dripping over the sides.

"Yes. I can notify them that you are allowed to visit." He turned his collar up as the wind became more insistent and the spray kicking off the water, heavier.

"Thank you. I'd like to go this week, please." Once I had reassured myself that George was none the worse for being manhandled by the police, I might be able to learn more about what Mr Novikoff and Lieutenant Dalton had planned.

"Why did you refuse his offer of marriage? Did you not want to be a queen?" Detective Archer's eyes twinkled with humour.

"No. While being Queen of England probably has much to recommend it, I couldn't imagine living my life with all those people watching me. Judging every move. I think such privilege creates its own sort of golden cage. I told George I am content with my quiet little existence. That probably makes me rather boring." Being royal and fabulously wealthy would be nice, but did it really solve all the problems in your life? Could a royal stand at the edge of a jetty and let sea spray soak their skin?

"You judge yourself rather harshly, just because you can see the hidden price others pay for their positions or choices." He turned and leaned on his elbow. The full force of that night-time gaze focused on me as he sought to peer into my depths and find...what?

I swallowed and watched a seagull trying to fly into the notorious wind, the bird not making any forward progress. I knew why I found myself lacking compared to others. Because my mother had. I so disappointed her, that she walked out one day and never returned. But that was a pain I wasn't ready to confront, and most certainly not with the detective.

"While everyone is so excited to see the prince, I can't shake the feeling that something bad will happen." My words were snatched away by the wind, and he had to lean close to hear me. "George confided in me that his entourage was keen for him to confront the prince, and I keep asking myself why they would do that. Was it something merely to amuse themselves and humiliate George, or did they have another motive?"

"A diversion," Detective Archer murmured so close to my ear, his warm breath puffed over my skin. "If George King had caused a scene, it would have given them a chance to do something else."

Like harm Prince Edward, I wondered.

"My men and I have been on alert for some weeks. We've heard whispers about the Irish protesters, but have no solid intelligence about the particular individuals who might be plotting something." He raised one hand, lifted his hat, and then rubbed at his temple before placing the fedora back down.

I made a decision, for better or worse, I would tell the policeman all I knew. "I know who they are. I saw two of them meeting George on Lambton Quay and recognised them. They were Mr Boris Novikoff and Lieutenant Sidney Dalton."

Dark eyebrows rose, which I took to mean they were names unknown in his investigation.

"A third man involved is Mr Sean Griffin. Adam

Dalton was seeing his daughter, Bridget Griffin. She's a friend of my assistant. They are both Irish and from what I understand, their fathers are very passionate about freeing Ireland from under the thumb of England. Mr Griffin escaped the Easter Rising but continues to campaign from afar." I danced along a fine line. Wanting to unburden myself, but always holding back the private thoughts and comments of others that I only knew by invading their memories.

He clenched his jaw. "I'm aware of the small segment of the Irish community who thinks disrupting the royal visit will force our government to do something to influence England. How do you think Mr Novikoff and the lieutenant are involved?"

I let go of a heavy sigh. Since he knew about the Irish lads, I could relieve myself of that burden. "Mr Novikoff blames King George for not saving the tsar and his family. He and his sister both feel the loss of their life in Russia, which they left as war broke out."

"That was unusual, for them to leave before the revolution and to come this far. Most of the White émigrés left Russia after the war, when Lenin took control."

"Miss Novikoff said their mother wanted to get as far away as possible, and they kept heading south until they boarded a ship to New Zealand. I understand they are less than impressed with how rural we are and the family longs to return to Europe." I clung to the tales my client told, of palaces of unimaginable beauty, balls where women dripped in diamonds and jewels, a lifestyle that seemed plucked straight from a fairytale. And then it all fell down and ended in a cold and bloody basement.

"Makes one curious what they were running from, doesn't it?" he mused.

I recalled Mr Novikoff's anger as he paced the parlour. "Do you think Mr Novikoff might do something in retaliation against Prince Edward?"

Detective Archer's short nails rapped on the wooden railing. "While I have men monitoring the Irish agitators, the Russian community is...problematic. It's a very small group and they are closed to outsiders. I cannot say how serious a threat they pose."

"Miss Novikoff came to me for a gown. She initially refused to attend any of the events, then at the last minute, she changed her mind and now wants to attend the ball. I have another client who will also be attending, on the arm of Lieutenant Dalton." Although I could not fathom the soldier's involvement other than loyalty to his deceased brother. The misfortune they had suffered in losing both parents most likely bonded them tighter together.

"You are uniquely placed, Mrs Devine. You are close to these women. It is possible you may hear something that gives weight to your concerns."

"You want me to spy on my clients?" Outrage surged through me and shook off the autumn chill.

"I am saying that if you suspect something that... troubles you... you have access to a set of confidential ears who will alleviate the concern for you." He had a way of phrasing it that made it sound like I would be doing my patriotic duty.

Yes, my mind whispered. At last, I can share what keeps me awake at night. My nerves had settled around the detective, and I decided he wasn't half bad as a wind shelter. Frank was too tall and lean, and the wind whipped around his narrow frame.

"So we have an Irishman, a Russian, and a New Zealander. An eclectic group of troublemakers to support Mr King's claim to the throne."

Or we had the start of a bad joke that my dad would tell. "Does this mean we are working together?"

The glint returned to his eyes. "It will make a change, will it not?"

Chapter Thirteen

Detective Archer telephoned my atelier later that afternoon and my breath hitched to hear his voice through the speaker. He had already arranged for me to visit George and enquired if I needed a ride. Not trusting myself to be in a confined space with him for the journey, I refused his kind offer. Then I telephoned Frank and imposed on him to act as my chauffeur.

Late Thursday morning, I sat in the Ford as Frank expertly drove us up the steep gorge road and over the hill to Porirua. I had been relieved to learn that George had not been imprisoned in some cold cell but sent to what was euphemistically called a residential home. One surrounded by a tall brick wall and with guards on the doors.

When we arrived and pulled to a stop before the iron gates, a man emerged from a little shed and questioned Frank through the wound-down window, before he admitted us. We swept up the drive with its immaculate lawns and the imposing house came into view.

"Are you sure about this, Gracie? He could be dangerous." Frank turned off the motorcar and cast me a worried gaze.

Burly men in white coats stood at the bottom of the front stairs as they smoked. They appeared ready to tackle anyone who tried to escape. Or perhaps to grab someone who should be kept inside. Like a woman who experienced another's memories when she touched someone. A woman whose grandmother had been labelled a witch, and who had passed down her tainted blood to her granddaughter.

The thought of danger for myself had never entered my mind until I stared at those white-coated men. Certainly, George would never harm me. I had known him for too long and had seen him continue to smile even as passersby hurled abuse at him. Whoever his father was, George certainly had a noble soul.

"George won't harm me. But you might need to break me out if those fellows decide I should be an inmate." I made a joke of the uneasy feeling in the pit of my stomach.

"Do you want me to come in with you?" Frank reached out and stroked the side of my neck.

I laid my hand on his arm. "No. George wouldn't be as chatty with you present."

"You know where I am if you need me. If you're going to jump out a window, give me a chance to get below it first." He grinned, and the tension eased.

Leaving the warm cocoon of the motorcar, I approached the house. The men gave me wary looks as I walked up the steps. I nodded and kept my chin high, as though I knew exactly what I was doing. Through the front door, I entered a small reception area. A woman with a starched white cap sat behind a desk. A pair of black-rimmed glasses balanced precariously on the very end of her nose. She glanced up at me.

"Yes?" She infused that one word with a world of suspicion.

"Hello, I have come to visit Mr George King. I have some scones for him if he is allowed them." I didn't bring a cake, even after Sam had joked she could hide a file in it. My so-called best friend also commented that if I made the cake, it would be an offensive weapon.

Her gaze narrowed at the paper bag. "Goods coming in need to be inspected. Are you a relative?"

I could have been George's queen, but given the surroundings, probably best not to announce I was unofficially engaged to the heir to the throne.

"I'm his cousin." The words stuck in my throat, but I managed to tell an untruth to the nurse. Thankfully, she didn't have the piercing stare that detected any lies like Detective Archer.

"You need to fill out the book." She turned the enormous tome in front of her around and pointed to a line. Then she held out a pen to me.

I took the pen and handed over the bag with four scones inside. With care, I wrote my name, the date, and the name of the resident I was visiting.

The nurse squeezed the scones in a way that would have earned her a slap from Sam. I only hoped the baked goods weren't too ruined when she handed back the bag.

"Visiting times are strictly limited to half an hour. We don't like our residents to be overstimulated." Then she waved over one of the orderlies who had come back inside. "Take Mrs Devine to see King, George."

I withheld my snort. By using the traditional British methods of surname first, Christian name last, the nurse gave life to George's belief he was royal—for she referred to him as King George.

"Thank you," I murmured as I followed the bulk of the orderly along a corridor. Moans and cries came from closed doors along the hall. At the end, it opened out into a large room that must have once been a grand parlour. Small tables were set up with puzzles and drawing materials. More white-coated orderlies stood in the corners like footmen, while nurses in their crisp uniforms hovered around the residents.

George sat in an armchair in the curved bay window, a closed book on his lap. He turned as I approached, a scowl on his face. Then it dropped away, and he beamed. "Mrs Devine! Have you come to rescue me?" He rose to greet me like a gentleman.

"I do have a getaway driver waiting, but I hear it is the convention to wait until a full moon, and we are supposed to tunnel out of the building and climb over the wall." I made a joke of any escape, in case the orderly decided I was a flight risk. Taking the seat opposite George, I handed over the paper bag. "I bought you some scones, as I know how much you like the ones from the Kostas Bakery. I am sorry, but the nurse *inspected* them."

George unrolled the top and pulled a slightly squished, inspected scone free. Then he rested the bag in his lap and laid the scone on top. "I am worried about Meg. Have you been to see her?"

Meg was George's horse and constant companion when he travelled the country. "Yes. I visited her up at the Arms and took her a carrot. She is well cared for and they know you are currently indisposed. They have promised to let me know if she needs anything, and there is a local lad who is taking her out for a walk each day."

He nodded, but worry lingered in his eyes. "I could not bear for anything to happen to her," his voice broke into a hoarse whisper. "Not after...what I had to do..." His gaze dropped to the scone in his hands.

I drew a deep breath. I knew a little about George's history. He grew up on a farm, like so many lads. When the call to war was made, he answered. As did his trusty farm hack. Thousands of horses were shipped overseas with the soldiers, but they never returned.

I reached out and took George's hand. "Meg is safe and cared for. Remember that."

He rested his hand on top of mine, but when he looked up, his mind was miles away and two years back. "What horrid, unfeeling little bureaucrat behind a desk thought we would repay our horses' loyalty and service by handing them over to be abused and worked to death. Far better a bullet from me than such a fate."

There were no words to ease the pain that George still felt. The stories of soldiers riding out into the desert and returning with only a bridle brought tears to my eyes. I rode the farm hacks but had never entrusted my life to an equine like George had done during the war. Nor had a horse ever wormed into my heart. I glanced at my wristwatch, aware the minutes were ticking by. Yet I was reluctant to bustle over the grief that still affected George at how he had to take his loyal companion's life.

"It was him, you know, I am sure of it," George leaned forward as he whispered the words to me. A rare vehemence in his voice and a gleam in his blue eyes.

"Who?" I'm fairly certain I knew who he meant, but I worried about the tone he used. George had never before displayed any anger towards the man he believed to be his half-brother.

"Edward. He served you know, in the army. They gave him safe assignments. Wouldn't do for the supposed heir to be hit by a stray bullet, but they trotted him around as though he was one of us. They even coined the nickname the Digger Prince for him." He scoffed and leaned back in his chair. "He's not a horse lover, you know. Prefers dogs. Little yappy ones."

The logistics of returning men and horses from war wasn't within my field of experience. But I could take a guess that legions of office workers scribbled numbers on an ocean of paper, trying to find how to do it with the ships available to Britain and her allies. Somehow, I doubted that the prince harboured some deep resentment from a pony standing on his foot as a boy, and retaliated by announcing that no horses were to accompany their riders back home.

Not being able to find the words to say, instead I squeezed George's hand and sent a hurried prayer to my gift to NOT show me those last few minutes he spent in the desert. It was hard enough to watch his despair. I wasn't strong enough to experience it as well.

Since George had brought the subject up, I continued the line of thought about his supposed royal relative. "I had wanted to talk to you about your half-brother. Or about him indirectly."

Only when I said the words did I glance at the orderlies. Would I be seized and dragged away for entertaining George's fanciful world? Regardless, I had to continue. Besides, Frank would break me out in a daring rescue if needed.

"You told me your entourage had a plan for you to meet. Can you tell me more about them and what they planned? Perhaps there is some way I can assist."

He huffed and broke off a large piece of scone and popped it into his mouth. Only once he had swallowed did he talk. "Good chaps, both of them. Boris is a bit strange, but he's not British so that is to be expected. Sidney is a true-blue supporter, and a Kiwi born and bred. His father hailed from England. He was a good man, too. Sidney told me the charges against him were untrue and trumped up to protect someone else. Someone high up in the ranks and poor Major Dalton was chosen as their whipping boy."

Questions were rabbits in my head. Sadly, they proliferated and then ran in different directions. I struggled to think which one to chase. I knew about Lieutenant Dalton's father. Frank had told me of the dishonourable discharge. Right now, the more enticing rabbit was the one called Boris.

"How did you come to meet Mr Novikoff?" Given the distaste he displayed for British royalty, I couldn't see him initiating a friendship.

"The lieutenant introduced us. The tsar was a cousin of King George, you know. His mother, my grandmother, was Alexandra of Denmark. Her sister, Dagmar, was the tsar's mother. It was a bad showing that my father didn't do more to save his cousin." George fell silent again.

I stared at the tips of my shoes. My visit seemed clothed in death and grief. Every turn of the conversation brought back restless ghosts from the war. The itch persisted at the base of my brain. There was something to learn here. "Do you know what they planned, George? How were they going to arrange for you to meet?"

He chewed another piece of scone, this one he savoured. He lowered his gaze and murmured from the side of his mouth. His mood seemed dark and gloomy, as though being stuck in the home had drained his natural enthusiasm for life that had always permeated his words and actions. Or perhaps old memories and wounds had overwhelmed his joy for this world. "They said it had to be somewhere open to the public since they couldn't get me an invite to one of the fancy events. Imagine, *me*, the true heir denied entry to Government House."

The prince had a busy schedule and in the three days he was in Wellington there were a dozen events crammed into every waking hour. "Did they say which one? He has such a hectic itinerary. I doubt the poor chap has time to dash to the loo, let alone have a quiet cup of tea."

George leaned back and screwed up his face. "No. We discussed a number of ideas. The lieutenant thought to make use of me being a soldier and slip me into the troop line-up at Newtown Park. I thought the children's display would be more fitting, out there on the lawn before Parliament. I could stride forth, tap Edward on the shoulder and declare myself the oldest son before a rapturous crowd." His tone increased as he spoke and an orderly detached from his position by the wall and advanced on us.

Having watched Theo practise the song the young children would sing during the display, I doubt anyone would hear George make his claim, even if he used a trumpet to amplify his voice. "I am glad you have more loyal friends than just me, George."

He tapped one finger to his chin and seemed lost in an alternate history playing out in his head. "Sidney says every son deserves to know his father. I only have photographs of mine. Over the years, I wondered why he sent my mother so far away and never wrote. I believe it is so I understood the struggle of the common man and it will make me a more understanding ruler."

The orderly narrowed his gaze and drew closer. His shadow loomed over me and a chill washed over my skin.

"I am afraid I must go, George. They seem quite strict about visiting time here. But I know you will soon be reunited with Meg, and I will have a wonderful cloak finished for you."

His eyes lit up with curiosity and his demeanour perked up to something more like the George I knew. "Will it have pockets?"

"Of course. Large pockets on the outside and secret pockets on the inside." I will admit I went a little crazy with the size and variety of pockets in the garment since I couldn't do it with most of the clothing I designed for my other clients.

He took my hand and pressed a kiss to my knuck-les. "Thank you, Mrs Devine, for being such a devoted supporter. Could you give Meg a big cuddle for me and scratch behind her left ear? She likes that."

I reassured him that his horse would receive ample scratches, then let the grumpy orderly escort me back through the building. Outside, Frank leaned against his motorcar and smoked a cigarette. He tossed the butt to the gravel and ground it with the toe of his shoe as I approached.

"All done?" Curiosity glinted in his eyes.

"Yes. I have been given the duty of scratching his horse's left ear. Thank you for bringing me out here, Frank. I appreciate it." I glanced back at the house and the bay window where George had sat, but his figure couldn't be seen through the thick glass.

"We Devines stick together. I'd never leave you in a place like this on your own." He held the door open, and I climbed inside.

Clouds gathered above the once grand house and the first patter of rain hit the windscreen. At least George was somewhere warm and dry—and out of harm's way. Whatever his entourage had planned, they were missing their distraction. But did that mean they would abandon their plans, or would they continue regardless?

Chapter Fourteen

Never had I been more relieved for a Friday. My team desperately needed a weekend for our fingers to recover. We had stabbed ourselves multiple times with pins and needles, as we rushed to complete every gown needed for the visit next week. I offered a silent prayer that no one had an accident with the lethal cutting shears.

I read the newspaper articles about the prince's visit as I chewed my toast. The actions of striking railway workers had caused a major disruption to the jam-packed itinerary. Unable to continue south from Rotorua, the prince was forced to turn back to Auckland until the dispute could be resolved. If necessary, he would travel on the HMS *Renown* to Wellington.

"No rest for the wicked," I murmured as I sipped my tea. The balls and dinners in Wellington might be delayed by a few days, but not postponed. Activities in the regions would be axed to make up the time. A shooting expedition in the Wairarapa would be sacrificed for the children's display on Parliament grounds.

As the clock dinged for half-past seven, I kissed Theo's cheek and grabbed my handbag and coat.

"I'll be home after five," I called out to Dad as I headed out the door.

Dad would walk his grandson to school so that I could start earlier. Today, Miss Novikoff would have the final fitting of her impromptu gown. As the clock struck eight that morning, I paced the reception area, with its honey-toned curved wooden desk. Mrs Mac had laboured for days on the beading, and I had promised her a bonus for completing the work. The client was expected at nine (although I was sceptical she would rise at such an early hour) and I needed to inspect the dress and prepare the fitting room.

Finally, the elevator groaned as it hauled itself to the first floor. The doors pulled back on Mrs Mac, a wicker basket clutched in her hands.

"Thank you for coming in early, Mrs Mac." I laced my fingers together to stop myself from snatching the other woman's basket.

"Jimmy is asleep, and the neighbour is keeping an eye on him for me." A tired and sad smile tugged at her lips. The injuries her son sustained in the war required full-time care, and Mrs Mac never complained about caring for an adult son as though he were a fractious baby.

"You know I am happy to sit with him one night if you want some time for yourself," I offered.

Nor, sadly, was she the only woman struggling to look after a permanently disabled soldier. Our governments sent our lads off to fight and never gave a thought to how to care for those wounded in battle. Not all injuries are visible. Joseph suffered, his scars on the inside, but men didn't discuss troubles in their minds. Not unless they wanted to be long-term residents of places such as where George now resided.

"Thank you, Grace, but we muddle through, and I do enjoy my time here when I am able to get away." Mrs Mac set the basket on the desk and removed a cloth-wrapped bundle. She opened one side to reveal the thick line of beading she had set around the neckline. The light played over the curve and the gown seemed ringed by flowing lava.

"Oh, that is marvellous! Let us hope Miss Novikoff appreciates all your work. I know I certainly do." I reached out and hugged her. I had poached the talented seamstress from The Cricket, where she had sewn the scandalous costumes for the burlesque dancers. That was also where she perfected her skill with beads, sequins, and tassels since the girls wore little more than that.

"I made beaded ropes that are knotted on the hip and fall over the train." Pride tinged her words, and so they should. Her work was perfection.

"I think this time, we won't dress a form in the fitting room. I don't want her to see the final effect until she turns in front of the mirror." The cool and elegant Russian woman seemed unmoved by anything our country had to offer, but I wanted to see if she would have the tiniest reaction to the final look.

Before I prepared for the imperious client, I had a much happier one to attend to. Mrs Taylor, my favourite fashion-forward client, arrived on the dot of half-past eight.

"Mrs Taylor, thank you so much for coming at this unreasonable hour," I said as I took her hand.

She dismissed my concerns with a wave of her hand and a snort. "I've been an early riser ever since I was a young girl working in a factory and never could get out of the habit."

"I can't imagine you as a factory girl." I had assumed the older woman had been born into money, not that she once worked for a living as I did.

She winked and chuckled as I showed her to the fitting room. "Oh, yes. Then I caught the eye of Mr Taylor, the son of the owner, and here I am." Then her smile faded away and pain flitted behind her eyes.

"How is your son?" I busied myself helping her out of her warm layers and into the gown for the grand banquet.

"Karl is learning some contrition now he has to work for a living, and I think it is doing him the world of good."

She turned her back to me so I could zip up the dress. Mrs Cooper loathed the new-fangled zippers, but Mrs Taylor liked the simplicity of being able to get herself into a dress. I added a piece of horizontal trim that concealed the metal teeth. Once done, I held out a hand to help her onto the low platform, then she turned to stare at herself in the mirror.

"I am glad to hear that. I think in this dress you are sure to be fending off politicians and diplomats at the banquet." The burnt orange of the silk was relieved by silver geometric lines. I thought she looked regal and fun at the same time.

"Oh, Grace, you have done it again. But I rather think I have given up on love. I don't think I am meant to be happy." She spun and the floaty fabric flared out around her.

"Nonsense. What happened to Richard was a tragedy, but it does not mean you are fated to be alone. You never know who is waiting around the corner." Perhaps the same applied to me. Once, I might have carved out a life with Frank, but now... I couldn't help but think I needed to keep walking and see what awaited me further along the path.

"Well, we shall see." She traced a shape with a fingertip.

With one client happy, and payment nestled in the lock box, I mentally prepared myself for the next.

When the elevator discharged its passengers, Miss Novikoff leaned on the arm of Miss Belmont. The Russian noble wore dark sunglasses and a hat with a broad brim, and I wondered if she had some affliction that made her allergic to sunlight. Not that there was much outside today.

In the fitting room, Miss Belmont reclined on the armchair and kept up a constant stream of chatter as I helped Miss Novikoff to change behind the screen. When she emerged, Miss Belmont stopped mid-sentence.

"Gosh," Miss Belmont said after a long and heavy silence. "You might never have graced the Russian court, Leena, but in that dress, I reckon you have great odds of being a British princess. I would be terribly jealous if I didn't have my Sidney. Assuming I can pull him away from the blasted radio he's always tinkering with to escort me to the ball."

Dress and client combined were stunning in a dark, seductive way. The beading flashed and drew one's eye to the flesh nestled next to it. The few tiny adjustments I had made at the seams meant the gown now fitted Miss Novikoff like a soft kid leather glove.

Inspired by Grecian robes, the silk clung to her form and tumbled in artful folds at the same time. The tasselled rope Mrs Mac made swung with a gentle clink at the side and highlighted the curve of the wearer's hip and thigh. I couldn't hide my smug smile of satisfaction that gown and client were a triumph.

Miss Novikoff stood on the platform and turned one way and then another before the mirrors. "It is acceptable. The next one will be beaded all over and not just these little bits." With one hand, she plucked at the dangling strand and examined the tiny rows of beads making up the tassel.

"I also lowered the neckline so your chosen necklace will have an inch of skin between the bottom of it and the top of the beading." Although it was only a tiny alteration to ensure the necklace would be on full display.

"Oh, honestly, Leena. It's bloody marvellous and if you don't say thank you to Mrs D and pay her a bonus for what she has done, then we can't be friends anymore," Miss Belmont said.

A long silence fell, and I stared at the toes of my shoes. Actions speak louder than words. Praise would be fabulous, but a bonus to share with my workers would be even better.

"Thank you, Mrs Devine. I will commission more outfits from you, and settle my invoice today," Miss Novikoff spoke without looking at me, her attention caught by her reflection in the large mirror.

Well, that was high praise indeed, given she thought everything in Wellington provincial and far beneath her noble nose. But I wasn't foolish, and I'd never turn away a client who settled their bill promptly and who looked so fabulous in one of my creations.

"It is a pleasure, Miss Novikoff. I am sure you will turn many heads. I do hope you will tell me, Miss Belmont, if Prince Edward dances the night away with Miss Novikoff."

"I won't need to tell you, Mrs D, their photograph will be in all the newspapers. I will be sure to tell the reporters that you made the dress." Miss Belmont spoke with her hands, dancing her fingers through the air.

Miss Novikoff muttered something in Russian under her breath, then she shook her head as though she had some disagreement with herself. "Boris insists that I must dance with this little prince. But, I..." she fell silent.

What would she have said, had she continued the thought? She didn't want to be involved in an assassination attempt?

"I didn't think your brother was particularly enamoured of British royalty," I ventured to say. If the siblings plotted something, now was my chance to learn more, while we were cloaked in the intimacy of the fitting room.

"He is not. It is some joke or other of his." She stepped down from the platform, and I held out my hand to steady her.

The memory was brief. A flash of an argument conjured by our discussion.

'No! I will not dance with him, or any of them!' I wanted to scream in frustration. Why did Boris not understand?

Boris loomed closer, his face blotchy with anger. Then he stabbed a long finger at me. 'You will do as you are told. Especially after all I sacrificed for you. We need you close if the other plan fails.'

Tears rolled down my cheeks. I would do as he asked, even though it meant killing a part of myself.

Then Miss Novikoff snatched her hand back and disappeared behind the screen.

I rushed to help so that she didn't pull on any of the delicate beading looking for the hidden closures. As I took the dress and held it over my arms, I couldn't help but wonder, what did Mr Novikoff plan to happen, once his sister slipped her hand into Prince Edward's and he led her to the dance floor?

For a few days, the city waited rather impatiently and officials hurriedly moved dates to accommodate the delays. Decorations were put up along the route the prince would take, only for the fierce wind to pull them all down again. Finally, late afternoon on Wednesday, the royal motorcade would roll into Wellington. The battle cruiser HMS *Renown* sailed into Wellington Harbour ahead of time and attracted its own curious crowd, eager to see the largest ship ever to visit New Zealand.

I collected Theo after school, as everybody who could make it would line the route. Dad grumbled about all the fuss, but he had a royalist heart. He took extra care when shaving, as though he thought the prince might touch his cheek! We all had our Union Jack flags to wave, and we discussed the best place to stake out our spot to wait.

"You are not to wander off, Theo." I pushed his thick hair to one side and then wedged his cloth cap on top.

We gathered at the end of Plimmer Steps, meeting Sam and her mother, Etty and her brother and, fleetingly, Joseph. My cousin was in his police uniform. The silver buttons on his jacket gleamed in the afternoon light, and his boots could have doubled as mirrors. I had never seen his uniform looking so clean and polished. All the police force would be on duty today, to ensure the royal visit went without incident.

"I can't stay," Joseph said, and his gaze lingered on Etty for a moment. "I'll be on the other side of Lambton Quay if you need me." He stared at me when he said that, and I wondered if Detective Archer told him that we were collaborating. Not that I had much to share apart from an unsettled feeling and a few stolen memories.

I nodded and placed my hands on Theo's shoulders before he darted after his uncle. We moved closer to the edge of the road and next to a lamppost with a solid base that Theo could climb. We had a good spot to see the motor vehicles roll down the street. The trams had been halted for the day. It certainly wouldn't do to have the prince's vehicle collide with a tram.

Patrick kept glancing around at the crowd and, at times, stood on his toes for a better look. I glanced from one sibling to the other. The niggle at the base of my neck whispered that Patrick was up to something.

"I'm going to stand with my mates. I'll find you later," Patrick said to his sister, then he dodged through the amassed people.

Etty sucked on her bottom lip, and I took hold of her arm. "He's in trouble again, isn't he?"

She nodded, and her eyes glistened with unshed tears. "Da and Mr Griffin are leading the young ones astray, I am sure of it."

Cold dread washed over my skin, and I shivered.

We'll only have one shot. "I have to stop them. I'll find Joseph on my way. Keep an eye on Theo, please!" With no time to say anything else, I dashed after the troublesome Irishman.

I ran across the road, nearly tripping over the tram lines when my heel caught in the track. Around the side of the fancy bank building, I found Patrick meeting up with two more familiar faces—the sons of Mr Griffin. The lads nodded to one another and then took off at a trot along a side road that ran parallel to Lambton Quay.

A sigh heaved through me. That morning, I hadn't dressed for exercise and there was no dignified way to run in a dress. Now I wished I had chosen trousers like Sam.

I followed the three lads as they headed down another lane, to where a motor vehicle was parked. Mr Griffin leaned against the side of the polished black metal. As the lads approached, he walked to the trunk of the car and opened the lid. Each man pulled forth something long and narrow and contained in a canvas bag, then flung the strap over his shoulder.

My brain compared a number of items to the shape of the bag. One dinged loud, triggered by memories of Dad, my uncle, and Joseph going hunting over the farm. They carried rifles to shoot the prince!

Chapter Fifteen

My heart hammered in my chest. If they aimed through the crowd, how many people might be accidentally hit? Or crushed in the panic once a shot rang out. I had to do something. My cousin was here, somewhere. I hoped I ran into him as I followed the men.

I stuck to the side of buildings, peering around the weatherboard side to keep track of the group. Fortunately, they didn't head back to the main road but appeared to have another destination in mind. They walked at a quick clip down another side street. All the while, I prayed to bump into Joseph.

I could run back to the main road to find help, but waving my arms and shouting was exactly what everyone else was doing. I would also lose sight of the men if I did that. The group approached the bottom of a three-storeyed building that overlooked the main route. Mr Griffin pulled a short piece of metal from his jacket pocket and stepped up to the door, hidden by the overhang. A crack sounded as he jimmied open the door.

The others looked around, and I ducked back behind the building, in case they saw me.

Think, Grace, think! Joseph had headed in this direction. Surely he must be wandering the side roads somewhere nearby. I drew a breath and wished I was like the little fantail, flitting above and able to chitter in a particular ear. One who listened to what little birdies told him.

As though summoned by my thoughts, Detective Archer and Joseph rounded the corner.

"Thank goodness." Relief coursed through me as I hurried to them.

"I was following Mr Griffin on your advice and met Constable Sullivan on the way." Detective Archer had the hint of a smile in his dark gaze.

"You have to be quick. They have gone into that building and they are carrying rifles!" I pointed at the shadowed doorway.

"Are you sure they are armed?" Detective Archer asked as we rushed towards the building.

"No. They are all carrying long, narrow canvas bags that look a lot like what Joseph and my dad store their rifles in." I wasn't entirely certain, but what else would they be carrying in the cases and why else make their way to a tall building that peered down on the approaching motorcade?

The two men rushed ahead, and I followed behind.

"Go for more help, Grace," Joseph said, and he gestured back towards the road.

"There's four of them and we have no time to lose." I pushed him into the darkened hall. Not that I would be any help. I saw myself in the role of offering moral support.

Before us was a long, narrow hall and to one side, a set of stairs. Footsteps rang out from the stairwell. Detective Archer didn't hesitate and began running up the stairs. Joseph stared at me for a long moment, then followed his superior.

I had no idea what I was going to do against armed men, but I could throw something or scream as a distraction. Upward we ran. On the last flight, the stairs turned into a narrow metal ladder that went straight upward.

"They're on the roof. Stay behind, Mrs Devine." Detective Archer reached for the first rung and climbed.

I was wearing a dress and had no intention of taking the lead, even if there weren't armed men above!

The hatch was unlocked and left open a scant inch. Detective Archer peered out. Then he carefully folded the hatch back, not letting it bang. His solid body uncoiled upward through the opening as easily and silently as a hot knife through butter.

Joseph followed with a practised ease. Then I remembered both men would have climbed up ladders to go over the top of the trenches when they charged at the enemy. I stood frozen with my hands wrapped around the metal of the top rail. What on earth was I doing? My idea to follow instead of running for help seemed rather foolish now.

Roars and yelling came from the road. The motorcade must have been spotted, as the prince travelled from the railway station to Government House in his convoy of slow-moving cars. The route was crowded with adoring subjects and showered with confetti.

The four Irishmen stepped to the edge of the roof, facing the street. They were spaced at an equal distance from one another. The noise from the excited crowd rolled up and over us. The prince couldn't be far away. This was what the Irishmen had meant in the pub that day when they said they had to time it just right. They needed the perfect shot of the royal personage. Vulnerable and exposed as he waved from his open vehicle.

Each man knelt down as he undid his canvas bag and reached within.

Detective Archer and Joseph exchanged a look. The detective made a hand gesture and then the two policemen sprinted towards the others. They had the element of surprise. Each tackled his opponent and took him to the ground. That left only two of the younger men—one of whom I knew.

I made a decision and sprinted from the ladder towards Patrick. As he looked up in surprise, I grabbed hold of the canvas bag and wrenched it free from his slack fingers. I tossed it to one side and glared at him.

"You have done it this time, Patrick Doyle. Etty will be ashamed."

"Ireland must be free!" he shouted, but he glanced around in an uncertain fashion.

"Then find another way to bring about change. Have you considered going into politics?" If I were his mother, I'd give him a good talking to. Violence was no way to solve problems.

He blushed bright red and his shoulders slumped. The sounds of the fight behind me were lost to the cheering and excitement from below.

The detective threw something metallic at me as he turned his attention from one fallen man to the last one standing. "Handcuff him please, Mrs Devine."

I caught the cuffs and stared from the man on the ground to Patrick. I shook a finger at Etty's foolish brother and told him to stay put. Then I approached the fallen man. He didn't appear to be moving. Somehow I managed to get the metal locked around his wrists while he moaned, but thankfully, he didn't rouse enough to resist my efforts.

The third lad fought on bravely, his arms circling as he tried to land a punch on the nimble detective. But soon, he too was subdued, like the others. Joseph shook his head at Patrick.

"You'll do jail time for this, Patrick. What will your sister say?" Joseph said as he placed handcuffs on him.

"We're fighting for Ireland!" Mr Griffin yelled from his spot on the ground.

"Bloody English!" his son Donald shouted from beside him.

The cheering went crazy below us. I peered over the edge to see the lead motorcar just nudging into view. Prince Edward, dressed in a dapper grey suit and hat, stood waving from the back of the lead vehicle. People waved Union Jack flags and strained for a glimpse of the royal heir. Confetti and streamers rained down as the motorcade passed. Some people were rushing at the vehicles, trying to get closer.

At least now it could pass without incident. I turned my attention back to the rooftop. Detective Archer approached one of the forgotten canvas bags.

"Let's see what we have here." He tugged the item inside free.

I frowned. What he withdrew didn't look like a rifle, but a bolt of fabric.

Detective Archer set it on the ground and gave it a shove. The fabric unrolled to reveal a long banner. Written in large letters, it said: FREE IRELAND.

The other bags contained more. One had an image of a red hand and underneath it read: NO HOME RULE. Another urged the British to GO HOME. The men weren't going to shoot the royal visitor but intended to use the prominent building to protest the situation in their home country.

I stared at the protest banners. "I feel somewhat foolish. I thought they were armed."

Detective Archer rolled a banner back up. "These are rifle bags and you had no idea what was inside.

And we have scuttled their protest. We'll take care of this lot if you wish to return to your family, Mrs Devine."

A conflict erupted inside me. This was my chance to wave at the prince, but would I make it down all the stairs before he reached our spot?

"I might watch from here. After all, it has a most excellent view." My hands curled around the edge of the building as the wind buffeted me. While a southerly had destroyed much of the bunting and plaster shield decorations that had been put up earlier in the week, several buildings were still covered in red, white, and blue, or topped with stars and crowns.

The motorcade pulled closer, the people below yelling wildly. The policemen on the street tried to hold back eager citizens. Those mounted turned their horses sideways, which created more chaos as the creatures blocked the view of those behind them.

People detached from the main crowd and rushed the vehicles. Some climbing onto the bonnet and running boards. A smaller figure darted between them, wearing a cloth cap on unruly hair.

"Theo!" I screamed his name, but no one heard me from above.

The child darted in front of the vehicle. It lurched to a sudden stop and in a horrible replay of what happened to Adam Dalton with the tram, I watched the child tumble under the wheels.

I screamed and almost jumped from the building in my haste. Detective Archer grabbed hold of me and spun me around. "Go," he said and gave me a gentle push towards the ladder.

Tears stung my vision, and I moved as quickly as I could. At the bottom of the ladder, I picked up my hem and ran. People surrounded the vehicles and police-men. I pushed them aside, using my elbows to muscle my way through.

A policeman tried to stop me. He placed two hands on my shoulders. "You can't go onto the road, ma'am. A boy has been run over."

"I think that's my son!" I tried to duck under his arm.

He narrowed his gaze and huffed. Then he let me go. I pushed closer, stopping at the edge of the crowd. The prince gazed down at the men in front of his motorcar. A frown pulled his brows together at the delay and commotion. An aide beside him spoke to him, and he nodded in response.

Two men gently lifted the boy from under the wheel. His cap fell to the ground and revealed light brown curls and a heart-shaped face. Not the black hair of the Sullivan family and our oval face shape.

"It's not Theo," I gasped, one hand shot to my mouth to stifle my cry of relief.

The boy still clutched his flag and waved it furi-ously at the prince, as he was carried to one side to allow the motorcade to continue on its way. A crying woman rushed to the little boy and grabbed hold of his hand.

I waited until the boy was taken away and the vehicles resumed their journey, then I crossed the road in their wake. Confetti littered the street like autumn leaves. Etty and my family still waited at the end of Plimmer Steps.

Etty rushed to me, worry in her eyes. What could I tell her?

"Patrick is in serious trouble this time, Etty. He could go to jail." I took her arm and tugged her into the shadow of the building with a modicum of more privacy.

Her mouth hung open for a moment, then she snapped it shut. "He's a bloody idiot! I've tried so many times to set him on the right path. I give up!" Her exasperation turned into tears and they rolled down her cheeks. "What will become of him now?"

"I don't know. I could perhaps ask Detective Archer." Not that I had any influence on him, but he might have an answer to the constant trouble that surrounded Patrick.

"Would you?" Hope burned in Etty's hazel eyes, and she gripped my hand tighter.

"I shall try. Did you think the prince was handsome?" I asked to change the subject.

A smile spread over her face. "He is quite dashing in person."

Arm in arm, we all headed back to my atelier for a late lunch. I had given my ladies the afternoon off. They had all worked so hard and they deserved some time to spend with their families. Etty was subdued, as worry about Patrick nibbled at her conscience. But I suspected her father would receive an earful when she got home. Sam and her mother had brought a basket of food from the bakery, and we sat in the airy workroom as we had afternoon tea and chatted.

After an eventful day, I was grateful to curl up in my armchair at home after dinner. The evening newspaper contained details of the prince's movements for the day. A tiny piece said the unfortunate boy had both his legs crushed by the royal vehicle, but the child remained in good spirits.

"Poor mite," I murmured as I drank my tea. A maternal instinct made me glance up and stare at Theo for a moment, playing with his soldiers on the rug. How easily it could have been him. A mother's life was a constant worry about how to protect her child from the dangers in the world. I hoped the tightness in my chest would ease as Theo grew older and learned how to spot trouble before he rushed into it. A lesson that Patrick Doyle obviously skipped.

The knock on the front door made me frown through the wide opening to the lounge. Friends and family used the back door. Frank entered unannounced. Who would use our front door?

"Who is that?" Dad asked from his armchair.

I set down my tea. "I shall find out."

As I approached the door, a shape loomed on the other side, shadowed by the soft light spilling from the house across the street. For a moment I wondered if it were some madman who would attack me, but then I doubted that sort knocked on the front door. Pushing aside foolish ideas, I grabbed the latch and opened the door.

Detective Archer stood on our porch. My brain stuttered to a halt.

"Good evening, Mrs Devine." He touched the brim of his hat.

My thought processes kicked back into action like Frank's Ford on a chilly morning. "Detective Archer. Hello. If you are looking for Joseph, he lives across the road." I pointed to the yellow cottage where Joseph boarded with Mrs Cox, the elderly widow.

"The constable sent me here. I wanted to talk to you if you have a spare moment." He slid the hat from his head and dangled it from one hand.

"Please, come in. Would you like a cup of tea?" From my experience of entertaining Joseph, most policemen appreciated a cup of tea and a biscuit.

He wiped his shoes on the doormat, then followed me into the house and closed the door behind him. "Thank you, although I can't stay long. I wanted to thank you for your assistance today. And for the invaluable tip to follow Mr Griffin."

"I'm glad they weren't armed with anything except protest banners." Only when I examined my behaviour from the comfort of an armchair and clutching a cup of tea did I realise how silly I had been.

We walked around Theo, occupying the middle territory on the rug, and entered the comfy kitchen with its armchairs at one end. Dad dropped his book into his lap. He had taken off his foot as he did in the evenings and had his legs up on the footstool.

"Dad, this is Detective Archer." I fetched a clean mug off the shelf.

Dad went to rise. The detective glanced at the foot sitting by the stool, and immediately reached down for Dad's hand and shook it. At the same time, he gently pushed Dad back down into his chair. "Mr Sullivan. Please don't get up, you look comfortable where you are. It's a pleasure to meet you, sir. Constable Sullivan is a credit to the family."

"So is Grace. She's not normally in trouble." Dad caught my eye, and I could see the concern written in his gaze.

"I assisted Detective Archer and Joseph today. I'm not in trouble, Dad." I carried the mug to the table and gestured for the detective to take a seat. Then I poured from the pot, kept warm in its blue-striped knitted cosy.

Detective Archer waved away the milk and scooped a large teaspoon of sugar into his mug.

Theo came and stood beside me, staring at the detective. His dark brows pulled in a disapproving frown. "You can't be here. Uncle Frank doesn't like coppers."

Chapter Sixteen

entrepreneur. I wasn't aware he lived at this residence."
Detective Archer's full lips quirked in humour before
he sipped the hot drink.

If the detective had crawled into every aspect of my
life when he believed I had murdered a client, of course
he would know that we were related to Frank. That
most likely explained why he regarded me with such
suspicion. Frank's illicit activities had coloured his
opinion. Did he think I likewise frequented darkened
alleys to make business deals? The idea of buying silk
from the back of a dirty truck made me shudder.

"You'd think Frank lived here, the way he walks in
without knocking," Dad grumbled from his chair.
"Serves him right if one day he swans in as I'm walking
back from the bath naked."

I nearly choked on my tea at the image Dad's words

conjured. "Frank leads his life following his own rules, but they are not necessarily how we choose to live." That was as close as I would come to criticising Theo's beloved uncle while he was listening. What I really wanted to say was Frank might be a minor criminal, but I preferred to keep my nose squeaky clean, officer.

"Uncle Frank says I don't have to tell you nuttin'," Theo said with a remarkably good American gangster accent he had probably picked up from one of Frank's *associates*.

"First, Theo, don't be so rude to the detective. Second, it's *I don't have to tell you anything*. Please don't slaughter the King's English. Why don't you go put your pyjamas on and get ready to continue your story with Poppa?" I brushed his dark hair to one side and then pushed him towards the stairs before he said anything else embarrassing. Or incriminating.

I waited until my son had started up the stairs before offering an apologetic smile to Detective Archer. "Sorry about that. Theo bounces between which of his uncles is his favourite at any one time. Currently, Joseph is on the outer, and he prefers his Uncle Frank." I suspected that with Anzac Day still recent in our minds, Frank had been telling Theo tales of his father and their exploits when they were younger. My son grabbed hold of any detail about his father. The war had stolen his chance to know Freddie for himself. Sadly, that also meant he had no chance to be disillusioned about his fast-living, womanising, petty criminal father. I would forever have to pretend he had been a wonderful man who hadn't broken my heart with his affair.

"I've had far colder receptions in my time." Detective Archer pulled me out of my reverie and back to Theo's attempts at giving the cold shoulder to the law. The man across from me sipped his tea and it might have been my imagination, but I thought his shoulders relaxed a little as he sat in our kitchen.

Staring at the detective reminded me of a promise I made to Etty. "What will happen to Patrick Doyle?"

He set down his mug and ran a finger along the thick handle. "The matter will go before the courts. It doesn't look good for him, not with his recent history."

I blew a waft of steam from the surface of my tea. If my gift wanted me to help Patrick, I struggled to see what else I could do. There came a point in life where all of us had to straighten our spines and dig deep if we wanted to change our paths. No one would do the work for us if we genuinely wanted something out of life. "He's a good lad, but sadly, easily led. We tried to push him under Joseph's wing, so he would have a better role model to follow."

Detective Archer stared off to the corner of the room as the cogs in his mind turned. Then he nodded to himself. "There might be something that can be done, depending on the judge who hears his case. Leave it with me."

We would have to cling to the faint hope of a way

out for Patrick. Or that the shock of realising he would go to jail might finally galvanise him into changing his ways.

"Are you off duty with an evening to yourself, since the prince has no engagements tonight?" I wondered what he did to relax. I imagined him hand washing his colourful handkerchiefs that peeked out of his jacket pocket. That image turned into the detective in his shirt and underpants and with garters holding up his socks, as he methodically ironed the squares of linen.

"Sadly, no. I must go and patrol Government House with the others. There'll be little sleep for any of us until the prince boards the *Renown* and heads to the South Island." Weariness tugged at the corner of his eyes, and he downed the rest of his tea and rose from his chair. "And I have taken enough of your time this evening. Thank you for the tea, Mrs Devine."

I followed him to the front door. "There is something else, Detective. Or it might be nothing, but George mentioned it when I visited him. He said Lieutenant Dalton had suggested slipping him into the troops for the inspection tomorrow as a way of confronting his half-brother."

Detective Archer made a humming noise as he considered that as a possible course of events. "If they were planning to use Mr King as a distraction, they have lost a crucial part of their plan. Possibly, they might try to insert a substitute if they are up to something and still need a way to pull attention away from their actions. Thank you, Mrs Devine. I shall be on the lookout tomorrow for Lieutenant Dalton."

Thursday dawned a fine and clear day. I read the newspaper articles about the previous day's events and couldn't decide if I was relieved or somewhat miffed, that there wasn't a single line about Irish protesters thwarted by a quick-thinking seamstress. Yesterday evening, the prince had made a speech at the town hall and declared that:

'I have long looked forward to the day of my arrival in this, the capital city of the most distant dominion of the king; but the reality has far exceeded anything which I was vain enough to expect. I can truly say that I have never had a welcome which has touched me more deeply.'

Today, the prince would kick off his whirlwind of engagements with the inspection of the troops at Newtown Park. Everywhere he went, there would be a focus on meeting war veterans and wounded soldiers. Soldiers would be lined up to see the man dubbed the Digger Prince. After the inspection today, the prince would be whisked off to a luncheon at Government House and the first of the two balls. Tomorrow was Theo's big day with the Children's Display at Parliament grounds.

The itch at the base of my skull refused to relent, even after George and the Irishmen had been detained. That left George's entourage—Mr Novikoff and Lieutenant Dalton. Were the two men still plotting some sort of disruption to the royal visit? Mr Novikoff's motive seemed clear. He blamed King George for not rescuing the Russian royal family. His angry words about how the British king needed to learn a lesson in loss and grief haunted my waking moments.

But what of the lieutenant? He seemed to flit at the periphery of events, yet I didn't doubt his involvement. His brother had died, whispering their time was near. The memory that rippled over my skin in those dying moments had been of the lieutenant pointing to a place on the map and saying, "This is where we do it." He could have meant the motorcade rolling along Lambton Quay, the event at Newtown Park, or another place.

My toast rebelled in my stomach as I considered the display the children would put on outside Parliament. Surely no one would plot anything that would put children in harm's way.

Pushing aside my fears for the youngsters, I wondered how deeply the two brothers were involved in any plot. Having met the charismatic Russian, I suspected both Dalton brothers were under his sway. The Kiwi men doing his bidding as he pulled their strings, manipulating events so that he could exact his revenge.

Since I couldn't breathe easy until Prince Edward boarded the *Renown* and sailed off to the South Island leg of his tour, I would attend the inspection of the troops at Newtown Park. Dad offered to walk Theo to school, so I could jump on an early tram out to the park.

"Are you sure you don't want to join the police force? You're certainly doing their work for them," Dad quipped as he made sure Theo had everything he needed in his satchel.

"I blame you," I muttered as I tugged on my coat. "This taint in my blood comes from your side of the family."

"Better a witch like your grandmother, than a hag like your mother," Dad replied, a hard glint in his eye.

He rarely spoke of Mum. The memories were too painful for him. Like Theo, I had no memories of my absent parent. However, in my case, she had willingly walked away from me.

I kissed his cheek. "I thought I was part sea monster, like you."

That replaced his frown with a smile. "You wait and see. Theo here will be a fine sailor one day and an excellent swimmer."

I didn't doubt it. Dad had a project in the shed at the rear of our tiny yard. When he had spare time, he quietly worked on a boat. Dad's hands lovingly crafted and shaped every timber in her. It would be a fifteen-foot yacht that he intended to use to teach my son to sail. Having sneaked in to see his progress, I suspected next summer would involve plenty of time out on the water. Once we had manoeuvred the boat out of the shed and past the house somehow!

"I'll see you at dinnertime." Having learned my

lesson from the previous day, I had dressed in trousers and a smart pale blue blouse under my coat. A close-fitting hat would defeat the wind and I thought made my entire ensemble rather smart.

My choice of outfit attracted a few curious stares as I hopped onto the tram, but channelling my friend's inner strength, I ignored them all. The world around us changed as we chugged into the twentieth century, and people would simply have to get used to women wearing trousers. They were ever so practical, and I enjoyed having the choice to decide for myself how I would tackle the day and dress appropriately. Not to mention that men's wear had far superior pockets.

I arrived at Newtown Park long before the prince was due. Tucked beside the zoo, the faint roar of lions and the chatter of monkeys carried over the treetops. On the grass in the centre, soldiers gathered in loose groups. They had polished their boots to a gleaming shine, and their uniforms were immaculate. They had creases in their trousers so sharp they could slice bread. Rifles with bayonets attached dangled at their sides. Officers yelled instructions, which were relayed by young cadets running back and forth.

The men were grouped in a ghoulish progression of the life of a soldier. Fresh-faced young recruits at the start of the line. Battle-hardened soldiers in the middle. The retired and injured on the far side. Orderlies unloaded carts and ambulances and then pushed bulky wheelchairs into place. A few of the men wore masks to cover their gruesome injuries suffered during the war.

Overseas, surgeons did groundbreaking work to fix broken bodies and broken lives. It was called plastic surgery, and I had read about it in the newspaper. There was a ghoulish interest in seeing how faces of the maimed were rebuilt and allowed men to walk down the streets without stares and whispers. Perhaps one day, such techniques will be available in New Zealand as our surgeons learned how to reshape tissue and skin.

I was wondering if one of the men in a wheelchair was Mrs Mac's son when I spotted her form fussing with the drape of a blanket over a man's knees.

"Hello, Mrs Mac. Lovely day for it," I said as I approached.

"Oh, hello Grace. Yes, I am pleased that the wind has died down a little." She fidgeted with the blanket even though there were no legs to cover up, and she glanced at her son. "This is Everett. My son."

"Pleased to meet you. I am very lucky to have your mother working with me." I smiled at the man, whose head rolled towards the sound of my voice.

The right side of Everett's face was covered with thick scar tissue from burns, and his right eye was a milky white. Apart from lacking legs, he was also missing his right hand and lower arm. His jacket was tucked up and pinned at the elbow. During the Great War, soldiers coined the term *basket case* to describe men so horrifically damaged and missing so many limbs that they were removed from the battlefield in baskets.

Everett muttered something in a low, guttural tone that had the rise and fall of a greeting.

Mrs Mac nodded and patted his shoulder. "Everett says hello. I wasn't sure about him coming out today, but they say the prince might talk to the injured men."

"I am sure he will stop and say a few words to you, Everett. To thank you for your bravery and for all you sacrificed for us." I addressed him directly, even though I couldn't understand his speech. But I laced my fingers together, not wanting to touch him and inadvertently see the mortar attack that stole his limbs and any chance of a normal life. "Do you have many former comrades here today?"

"Oh, yes. They have promised to take good care of Everett today." Mrs Mac curled her hands together, and worry wound around her.

I met Everett's one good eye and leaned closer. "Do tell me what the prince had to say afterwards. You will be the envy of every young woman in Wellington once you have spoken with him."

His shoulders heaved, and he made a wheezy attempt at laughter.

I patted Mrs Mac on the arm. "Why don't we have a cup of tea afterwards and leave Everett to have a beer with his mates?"

She glanced at her son, and the refusal was on the tip of her tongue. Poor woman. Everett needed constant care, and her motherly duties would never be over. Did she fret about who would tend to him when she couldn't anymore?

Everett made another noise and gestured with his

good hand towards a particular group of soldiers. One raised his hand in response.

Mrs Mac's features softened. "All right, then. But they better not get him drunk."

We organised a spot to meet, in case we lost sight of each other as the crowd grew. Then I wandered along the crease of a hill, watching the soldiers. All the while, the niggle at the base of my skull itched worse than a mosquito bite.

Chapter Seventeen

Each minute that passed, more and more people flowed into the park, picking spots on the gentle slope where they could see the proceedings. A temporary grandstand had been erected to one side, where the invited dignitaries, politicians, and the wealthy would sit. Mrs Cooper might be among them if she overcame her reluctance to rub shoulders with the British nobility once more.

I circled the crowd, popping up on my toes as I scanned faces and tried to pick out the cuckoo among the hundreds of soldiers. Then I reminded myself that Lieutenant Dalton was a soldier, not an outsider. He would be here, somewhere. Since there was a smaller number of officers, he should be easier to discern. They also wore a different uniform.

A tingle ran along my limbs, and I couldn't dismiss the sense of impending disaster. Some of the soldiers broke ranks and adopted relaxed poses as there was still no sign of the prince. As I pretended to search for a spot to sit, I continued my inspection of the troops.

My heart leapt when I recognised a familiar face under the peak of a cap. Lieutenant Dalton. He smoked and chatted with another lieutenant not far from a company of men. A glance at the badge on his cap with its five-pointed star flanked by fern fronds meant he was part of the 17th (Ruahine) Company.

I set a determined path for him, while my mind whirled with what to say. I could hardly demand to know if he meant any harm to the prince. Not that he would answer honestly, even if he was a participant in such a plan. Words lied. But memories seldom did.

That thought halted my feet for a moment. Never before had I intentionally used my gift, but I couldn't imagine a greater need. I carried on, an idea unfurling inside me.

The conversation of the officers halted as I appeared beside them, and I swallowed my nerves as they all turned to stare at me.

"Good morning, gentlemen. Do excuse me, but could I have a quick word with Lieutenant Dalton? I have a critical fashion question to ask him."

The other lieutenant chuckled, but Lieutenant Dalton scowled, words of dismissal forming on his lips. Before he could tell me to go away, I reached out and grabbed his hand just above the wrist.

"Are you aware that Miss Belmont's gown will be a deep shade of pink? I hope your evening attire won't clash?" As I said the words. I formed a different question in my mind. *What do you have planned?*

"I know Fleur loves pink and I am informed black goes with everything." He shook his arm and broke free.

But not before the brief memory ran up my hand, along my arm, and jolted into my brain.

He picked the pocket watch up from where it sat on the table next to the radio. He held it in his palm and his thumb rubbed over the bullet hole. 'The time has arrived. We're going to get the bastard, Dad. This is for you.'

The flustered look on my face didn't need feigning. "Of course. How silly of me," I gushed. "It's just I want everything to be perfect for Miss Belmont. Good day, gentlemen."

It had worked. Sort of. The officer was indeed up to no good, motivated by the memory of his father. Not that my gift had shown anything of value, and merely confirmed what I had already suspected. Blast. Why couldn't it be useful and show me exactly what the men intended instead of being limited to what had already happened?

Marking the lieutenant's location on my mental map of the park, I carried on. If the puppet was present, somewhere would be the man pulling his strings. Not too much further along, one soldier stood apart from the other troops. His lonesome stance seemed unusual when men grouped in clusters of three or more to trade cigarettes and stories. I stared at the soldier. There was something familiar about his build and appearance. His lemon squeezer hat was tugged low on his brow, and it took long seconds for my mind to scan my memories and dig up a name to attach to his profile.

Boris Novikoff.

As far as I knew, he hadn't served in the army. Or at least not the New Zealand forces. So what was he doing dressed as one of our boys? The bayonet at the end of his rifle glinted in the sunlight as he turned and made eye contact with me. His eyes narrowed as recognition flowed between us. Hopefully, he would dismiss me as only a seamstress, without any inkling of his horrible plan. From the way he clutched his rifle, I suspected his intention was to do to Prince Edward exactly what the Bolsheviks did to his tsar.

I had to tell someone. Given the Russian's attire, he was substituting himself for George King in the line-up. Although not as a diversion, but so he would be close to the prince to strike out with his weapon. As I considered who to alert, Mr Novikoff slipped behind a group of men gathered in a circle. I spun around, searching for Detective Archer. He was here. Somewhere.

My heels sank into the soft grass as I hurried along the rows of soldiers. It seemed to take an eternity to spy the detective, clad in his army uniform of khaki rather than his usual suit. His cap was adorned with a rampant lion standing on a coronet, the symbol of the 7th (Wellington West Coast) Company. He talked to another officer in the same company.

I rushed over and tapped his arm, rudely interrupting his conversation. "Excuse me, Detective Archer, but what we discussed last night seems to be unfolding. Lieutenant Dalton is over with his company, but Mr Boris Novikoff is here also, and dressed as a soldier."

His body tensed, alert to danger. He dismissed the other man and turned his full concentration on me. "Where is he headed?"

In finding the detective, I had lost sight of the fake soldier, and I held back a frustrated wail of *I don't know!*

"He was standing off to the side of the troops and all on his own. Then he slipped behind a group of men when I believe he recognised me. But he has no way of knowing that I am aware of his plan. He is carrying a rifle, Detective Archer, one with what appears to be a very sharp bayonet in place." Yesterday I saw rifle bags and jumped to the conclusion they held firearms. What they had actually contained was rolled-up banners. This time I had no doubt that the conspirator carried a weapon.

From a distance, soldiers in uniform all resembled one another. You had to pay attention to discern the differences in height, build, and then profile. Only when close could you pick out the different insignia on their hats and sleeves.

"He will be hiding to bide his time. Once the troops are all assembled, he can easily slip among them." Detective Archer scanned the grounds. On one side, a grandstand had been constructed for officials and invited guests to have a better view of the proceedings. Only the bottom rows were filled so far, the others either had not yet arrived or were waiting until closer to the time that the prince would appear to find their seats.

"What of Lieutenant Dalton?" We had two men to keep track of, and they were in different directions.

"I'll alert Constable Sullivan to keep an eye on him and send out the word about Novikoff." He scanned the faces, searching for his constable.

"We should split up. Two of us can search for Mr Novikoff quicker than one." We knew a general direction, and surely it wouldn't take too long to flush him out.

He clenched his teeth together at my idea. "Split up? You are not going after him at all, let alone by yourself."

"I am surrounded by dozens of soldiers and the constabulary. If I see him, I will grab the closest man to assist." A park filled with hundreds of soldiers struck me as the safest place to pretend to be bold.

Concern burned in the detective's eyes, and I stood a little taller and held my shoulders straight. He could waste time telling me to go and sit on the grass, or simply get on with it. He let out a huff but decided on the latter. "Very well. I'll inform my men to keep watch, but we don't want to start a panic. We should be able to take him down quietly, without anyone aware of his presence."

Just as we did with the Irishmen and their banners. Although no one had been at risk of an injury from rolls of fabric.

We both hurried in the same general direction. The detective veered off to talk to Joseph, also in his khaki uniform. No doubt my cousin would relay the word to the other policemen among the soldiers and set some to stand watch over Lieutenant Dalton. Although the instructions about Mr Novikoff would be vague. What did Detective Archer say, look out for the soldier carrying a rifle? There were so many of them.

Pushing that aside, I carried on to where I had last seen Mr Novikoff. From there, I scanned the closest faces, looking for the distinctive nose and darker skin tone. Men were making their way to their final positions, and I threaded through them, muttering excuse me and sorry as I peered into faces.

"This is hopeless," I muttered to myself as I swam in an ocean of khaki. They all looked the same.

Those words echoed through my brain. Exactly! I need to look for what didn't fit. Who is different and gives off an air of not belonging? Not in appearance, but in their actions. With that idea, I cast around again. There was an easy camaraderie among men who had lived and fought together in the trenches. Something the cuckoo among them couldn't mimic.

With eyes unfocused slightly, I let my gaze drift over the soldiers and whispered to whatever lurked in my blood, to do something useful for a change. Whether the magical taint dinged in my head, or if he gave himself away by not fitting in with the other soldiers, my eye settled on one figure at the edge of a laughing cluster.

"There you are," I whispered and set off at a determined pace straight towards him.

He glanced around as I bore down on him, and he took off at a trot behind the grandstand. Did the detective follow and spook him? Surely one seamstress wasn't reason to give flight. Without pausing to look over my shoulder, I hurried after Mr Novikoff. The surrounding crowd surged forward, eager to catch a glimpse of the prince as word went up that the motorcade had been spotted. It seemed as though I fought my way through a torrent of water. Finally, I made the outer edge of the mass of people. As I rushed towards the wooden structure, a hand latched onto my arm and stopped my forward progress.

A tingle ran up my arm from the contact through the light fabric of my blouse and fluttered through my torso.

Mutu! An elderly voice called from inside my head.

I didn't know what the word meant, but my feet wobbled to a stop and turning, the worried eyes of Detective Archer regarded me. "Mrs Devine, it is not safe to tackle him alone. You promised to grab the closest soldier if you spotted Mr Novikoff."

I grinned at him. "I just have." Telling my gift to stay quiet, I slid his hand down to mine and tugged him towards the temporary structure.

I didn't care if it was safe or not, I needed to find

out what the men were going to do. Before I could open my mouth to make another comment, a rumble travelled through my feet and up my legs. My brain cried out *earthquake!* Then the scream of splitting wood and the crash of metal assaulted my ears.

A cloud rolled over me as the ground rushed up to greet me and the sky went dark. Was it a bomb?

I cracked one eye open, expecting to see fiery debris raining around us. Instead, I stared into the handsome face of Detective Archer just three inches from my nose. His cap was askew, and I reached up with one hand to correct the angle. He had flung me to the ground and covered my body with his rather solid one. My breath came shallow in my chest, as I tried hard not to breathe as each exhale pressed me tighter against him.

"Was it a bomb?" My voice was shaky and my heart pounded. If anyone knew what a bomb sounded like, it would be the captain. Now I wondered how they didn't all have shattered nerves going through a multitude of such explosions every day.

"No. Are you hurt?" he asked, letting go of his tight hold on me.

Only now did I realise that his arms were around my body and he must have used them to soften my fall somewhat. "Only a little winded from colliding with either the ground or you. What happened?" Most likely, it was his solid chest that had stolen my breath.

He pushed off the grass to stand, then offered his hand to help me to my feet. "The grandstand collapsed.

I must see if anyone is hurt and find Novikoff." Once he saw I was upright, he let me go to disappear into the dust cloud.

Cries came from those who had been seated in the grandstand. I brushed grass from my clothing. Dust drifted across the park until it met the breeze rolling off the harbour. At which point, it was swiftly dispersed in a multitude of directions. Shouts competed with the noises from the zoo. As the dust cleared, it became obvious what had happened. Just as the detective had said, the temporary grandstand had collapsed.

Luckily, there were hundreds of soldiers present who leapt into action with military precision. Uniformed men helped those who had been seated at the front of the collapsed structure free of the wreckage. Fortunately, there were also medics present with their ambulances to tend to the injured. With nothing I could do to help, I instead focused on searching for Mrs Mac. As a mother, I guessed she would make a beeline for her son as soon as the crash sounded.

I headed for the injured men and the collection of wheelchairs and stretchers. Sure enough, Mrs Mac hovered around the men like a protective mother hen.

"Is everyone all right?" I called out, hoping the men were far enough away from the grandstand and any flying debris.

"Yes. Only a little dust on them and the wind will soon blow that away," she answered.

Once I had reassured myself that the wounded hadn't been further wounded and that my sequin magician had matters well in hand, I turned my attention back to Mr Novikoff.

My heart clawed its way up my throat as a dusty body was carried from the pile of timbers, supported by a shorter but more solid figure.

Chapter Eighteen

ANOTHER SOLDIER RUSHED FORWARD and took hold of a limp arm, swinging the limb over his shoulders. The injured man's head drooped forward and he no longer wore his distinctive hat. Nor did he carry a weapon. The toes of Mr Novikoff's boots dragged through the grass as if he had no control over his lower legs.

Two more soldiers approached, carrying a stretcher between them. Lowering the canvas to the ground, the medics manoeuvred the tall Russian onto the stretcher as the two men supporting his body lowered him. His body was so still, I assumed he had perished in the accident. Then his chest heaved in a sudden indrawn breath.

"What made the grandstand collapse if it wasn't a bomb?" I asked the detective once he had seen Mr Novikoff stowed in the ambulance.

He removed a handkerchief from his pocket and

used it to wipe dirt and sweat from his brow. He must have waded into the wreckage to pull the Russian free. "I don't know. But it was rather spectacular bad luck for Mr Novikoff that it did so as he hurried underneath it. It was lucky that you had not run in after him."

It wasn't lucky. The old woman's voice had called out and my feet had halted in response. "Will he survive?"

The ambulance rattled over the turf to reach the drive and then disappeared around the curve of the hill.

"He's unconscious. We'll know more once he is examined at the hospital. It seems that once again, you have thwarted an attempt on the prince." Humour shimmered in his dark eyes.

"I'm not sure yesterday counts since they were only armed with banners, not bayonets." An old saying that Dad often muttered when something failed ran through my head, *third time lucky*. If we counted the protest by the Irish lads, and today...did that mean if someone still remained to carry out their plot, that tomorrow they would be successful? I didn't like that idea.

"What happened to Lieutenant Dalton?" Only now did I realise one man was still at liberty.

"He's with his company. If he had any part to play in whatever Mr Novikoff planned, he never made any move." Detective Archer scanned the soldiers and his attention alighted on one in particular. "But I shall keep him under watch."

The detective left me to help with moving the politicians and guests to another, still upright, set of seats. When the cheering started, I quickly vacated the grounds as the men snapped into lines and found a spot on the grassy bank to sit and watch.

After an eventful morning at Newtown Park and a lovely lunch with Mrs Mac, I took a tram back to my premises. With a mug of tea in my hand, I settled in the quiet of my office and stared out the window at the gathering clouds. I remained determined to finish the cloak for George and had the pile of woollen cabbage all pinned and ready to sew the liner.

I decided that would be my afternoon task. It wouldn't take me too long to stitch together the patchwork. Then I could shape it to the waxed cotton outer that was draped over a dress form. How long had it been since I settled at the Singer sewing machine and concentrated on simply...sewing? It felt like a lifetime but was probably no more than a few weeks.

For me, there was a peaceful, meditative quality to sewing. To lose myself to the fabric in my hands and the whirl of the machine. Watching each stitch formed by the pass of the needle. Even ironing had its own rhythm, as I heated the iron, and pressed the seams open. By the time I turned off the lights for the evening after everyone had gone home, the cloak was almost finished. The question of did it have enough pockets could be resolved tomorrow.

"How was your day, love?" Dad asked as I walked

in the back door and placed my bag on the bench under the coat hooks.

"The grandstand collapsed at Newtown Park. Luckily, no one was killed and only one man was taken off in an ambulance." My coat came off next, and I shook it out before hanging it up.

"Crikey! What about Prince Edward, was he hurt?" Dad placed the kettle on the range and fetched down a mug from the cupboard.

"It was before he arrived. The inspection went off without a hitch. He chatted with the wounded for quite some time and then he made a lovely speech at the end." He did have an eloquent turn of phrase, but then someone else probably penned every word he uttered.

What did he write in private, I wondered? Would I be fascinated to know what thoughts he committed to paper, only to be seen by his family or perhaps a lover? Or would I be horrified to learn what he really thought of New Zealand and his reception here? I pondered the dual nature of life as a royal as I nursed the mug of tea and munched a biscuit.

After dinner, I kept one ear on the radio as Theo went through a last-minute rehearsal. The news reported on every move the prince had made during the day, and only briefly touched on the collapse of the grandstand. My attention kept drifting to the front door, and I finally admitted to wondering if Detective Archer would pay another visit to thank me. Or most likely, he couldn't get away from his official duties to prowl the grounds of where the prince was being entertained.

Friday morning dawned crisp and clear, and I had one less thing to worry about. At least Theo wouldn't be saturated by rain as he performed. Today was my son's big moment—the children's display on the lawn outside Parliament. With a heavy heart, I watched him join his classmates, worry nibbling that he might become lost among the hundreds of people expected to attend. The teachers were responsible for marshalling them down to the grounds and back again. They weren't going far and Theo knew his way home if he became separated from his group, I reassured myself.

We would all go and watch. Although I doubted if we would be able to find Theo's happy face among the hundreds of other children from our spot on the outer edge of the lawn. I chose to settle by a tree, so Dad could lean on it for support if needed. The children laughed and screeched as they were organised into rows.

Rows of girls in straw boaters and smart pinafores lined one side. They waved their Union Jack flags as the prince stepped from his motor vehicle. While neither tall nor broad, he possessed a certain dashing quality. Or it might simply have been the romance of him being heir to the British throne that enhanced his attractiveness.

The prince smiled, waved, and shook small, outstretched hands on his way to the sheltered platform where he would sit for the performance. Thankfully, the speeches were kept short. No one wanted hundreds of bored and restless schoolchildren!

I sang along under my breath as the youngsters belted out the songs. Dad placed one hand over his heart as they practically shouted the words to 'God Save the King'.

"Prince Edward won't hear another performance like that anytime soon," I said as the event came to a conclusion and the heir was ushered back to his waiting vehicle.

"He won't be hearing anything for at least a week, I reckon," Dad chuffed.

Once the royal visitor left, chaos washed over the grounds. Children darted in all directions and teachers tried to wrangle their charges back to classrooms. Overcoming my earlier fears, I gladly left others in charge of ensuring my child was collected and herded towards Thorndon.

Dad and I parted ways. He would slowly make his way around the Parliament grounds and collect Theo on his way past the school. I doubted any of the children would be able to concentrate on schoolwork this afternoon, after their exciting morning. The Thorndon School teachers, no doubt realising the same thing, had said they could go home once they returned to the school grounds.

Tucking my bag under my arm, I marched towards

Lambton Quay. Despite the festivities happening across Wellington, work continued in my atelier. We were well advanced on spring outfits for later in the year, for those of my clients who liked to be ready on the first day of September.

Afternoon lengthened when I decided to review what bolts of fabric we had in the storeroom. My memory needed a refresh, as often a particular pattern or colour would influence the designs I drew. As I walked down the short corridor, the elevator shuddered to a stop and the ornate metal doors slid open to reveal Miss Belmont.

I approached my client and wracked my brain to recall if she had an additional fitting scheduled that I had forgotten.

"Miss Belmont, how lovely to see you. How is Mr Novikoff?" Joseph had informed me that he had suffered broken ribs and a nasty injury to the head, which caused his bout of unconsciousness.

"He will live, but he had better enjoy his respite in hospital, as I am sure they will cart him off to prison. I can't believe how stupid he was! To think he intended to bayonet the prince." Her hand went to her heart in horror and her eyes widened.

I shared her disbelief at what he intended but was sceptical if he would ever see the inside of a jail. It was a sad indictment on our society that the incredibly wealthy rarely paid for their actions. Although some would argue the collapse of the grandstand had been some divine intervention in his plans. That made something Lieutenant Dalton said rattle around in my head. People should be held accountable for their cowardly actions.

"It seems he was rather passionate about the deaths of the Romanov family," I murmured. Had his sister now been freed from whatever obligation he had exerted over her? I ventured a question that nibbled at the edges of that. "Does Miss Novikoff share her brother's views?"

Miss Belmont snorted. "No. If anything, I think she is somewhat relieved that Boris is now indisposed." She leaned in closer and dropped her tone to a conspiratorial whisper. "Boris was pressuring her to seduce the prince. Can you imagine that?"

"It wouldn't be a difficult task, in my opinion, with how she looks in the red gown." The Russian woman embodied seduction in the way the silk clung to her body.

My client tapped my arm and laughed. "Oh, too true, Mrs D. But Leena has no interest in the prince. Boris had some hare-brained scheme about her marrying Prince Edward and becoming queen. Then he thought the two of them could command the British Empire and its armies to free Russia from Lenin. Mad. Utterly mad." She waved her hand as though mosquitoes buzzed all around her head.

"If that was his goal, why then did he go to Newtown Park disguised as a soldier with the intent of harming Prince Edward?" Why assassinate the man you wanted your sister to wed? That didn't make any sense.

"Apparently, Leena dug her toes in and told Boris in no uncertain terms that she wouldn't do it. He must have changed his mind at the last minute." A frown wrinkled her delicate skin as she tried to imagine what had motivated her friend's brother.

"Well, now she is free of that obligation and may enjoy the ball and seduce whoever she wants." If the fates wanted to smile on me, a photograph of Miss Novikoff in her Grecian gown on the front page of the *Dominion Post* would do fantastic things for my business.

"Anyone she smiles at tonight will be instantly smitten, I am sure," Miss Belmont said in a wistful tone.

"Speaking of tomorrow's ball, I hope there is no problem with your gown that brings you here?" I tried to nudge the conversation along.

"Oh, no," she gasped. "I've come to collect the clutch."

Of course. We had made a tiny beaded bag to match her gown.

"Forgive me. In all the excitement, I forgot about it." I walked to the large kauri cabinet that sat behind the desk. Dad had lovingly carved the piece and added the frosted glass panels to the upper cupboards. Soft smears of colour were visible, but not the exact items stored within.

I lifted down a small bundle carefully wrapped in a soft cotton bag. Easing a hand inside, I removed the pink beaded clutch from its protective outer and showed it to Miss Belmont.

"Oh, that is gorgeous." She took the tiny bag and held it to the light.

Mrs Mac had beaded the entire thing in pink, cerise, and cream beads. We made it only as large as it needed to be, to hold lipstick, a compact, and a handkerchief.

"I'm glad you like it. Might I suggest keeping it in the cotton bag when you are not using it to protect the beads, and the fabric will gently buff them to keep them shiny." I held open the cotton bag, and Miss Belmont slid her clutch inside.

Pulling the drawstring tight, I handed it over. "Will Lieutenant Dalton be accompanying you tomorrow?"

She blew out a snort. "If I can drag him away from that stupid radio."

I recalled the flash I had seen the previous day when I touched his arm. A radio sat on the table beside the pocket watch. "Oh? Is he following all the news reports of the prince's movements?"

"Yes and no. He's hanging on every word of the prince's like a smitten debutant. But no. This is some stupid broken radio that Boris gave him. Honestly, that man is obsessed with the thing. I have been to his house, and he has one already. Why would he need two?"

I shook my head. "I'm afraid I don't understand the things that men fixate on."

"Well, thank you Mrs D. I shall go and start the

process of making myself beautiful for tonight's dinner." She grinned and tucked the cloth bag to her chest.

"I'm sure that takes no time at all, Miss Belmont," I murmured as I escorted her back to the elevator.

That night, I curled up in my favourite spot clutching a mug of tea and let the events of the last few days swirl through my mind. The itch remained, but the visit was coming to an end. Soon, Prince Edward would sail off into the horizon, and I could let out a long-held breath.

Our time is here.

A pocket watch with a bullet hole in it.

A major posthumously dishonourably discharged.

An angry man adamant people pay for their actions.

All the pieces came together in my mind. Only a few spots were missing to make the whole. What was it that George said to me when I visited him in the residential home? Something about how Lieutenant Dalton believed that charges against his father were untrue and trumped up to protect someone else. That Major Dalton was the whipping boy.

We're going to get the bastard, Dad. This is for you.

Oh. Crikey. Just as everything snapped together, a rap sounded at the front door.

"I'll get it." I moved as though in a dream, my brain staring at the mosaic that appeared in my mind. Finally,

I could see the complete story. I flung open the door without really looking, to find that Detective Archer once again stood on the porch.

"Oh, you. Brilliant!" I gushed to exactly the person I needed to talk to. "It's been Lieutenant Dalton all along."

Chapter Nineteen

A slow smile spread over Detective Archer's face. "I came here to tell you the same thing."

I gestured for him to come inside and bustled him to the kitchen. The detective greeted Dad, who read in his usual spot, while I made two cups of tea and considered how to phrase what I knew. Blurting out that I had a weird magical ability, which saw Sidney Dalton vow to make the prince pay for his father's demotion, wouldn't work. Instead, I considered what was more easily shared, that made more sense once I considered the memory snatched from the brief contact. "George King told me that the lieutenant believed the charges against his father were unfounded, and that he was made the whipping boy to protect someone higher up. A whipping boy took the punishment for a noble. Or a royal. Lieutenant Dalton believes Prince Edward was the one who gave the orders in that disastrous campaign."

The detective waited until I sat before taking the chair opposite me. He spooned sugar into his cup and stirred with a slow motion. "I have been looking into the history of the Daltons at war and the circumstances of Major Dalton's dishonourable discharge."

My fingers slid through the handle of the mug, and I tightened my grip. "Was Prince Edward responsible for the disastrous campaign?"

He sipped his tea and regarded me over the rim of his mug. "He was stationed with Major Dalton but never made any tactical decisions. I think some would call the prince's presence as more show pony than workhorse."

Dad snorted from behind his book at that analogy.

"It can't have been easy to live with the disgrace his father's actions brought upon the family," I murmured. In some ways, I could understand him creating the tale of his father being a scapegoat to ease his family's suffering.

"From my enquiries, the lieutenant convinced himself that Prince Edward gave the crucial command and that his father was sacrificed as part of some cover-up. But I cannot find a scrap of evidence, or even a whisper, to substantiate that." He took a large drink from his tea and glanced at his wristwatch.

He looked tired, and I wondered how many hours of sleep he managed to grab before he had to rise and watch over the Prince of Wales once more. A duty that would soon be discharged. "The prince is only here for one more day, and you are down to the last conspirator."

"That is partly why I am here, Mrs Devine. To once again call on your assistance. I cannot locate Sidney Dalton. He's not at his flat and seems to have gone to ground somewhere. Is it possible he is with your client?"

I shook my head and placed my mug back on the table. "Miss Belmont lives with her parents, and I cannot see them allowing her beau to stay under their roof."

"Then my men and I shall be extra vigilant tomorrow. You would be best advised to stay away, Mrs Devine. We don't know what he might be capable of."

He finished his tea, and I walked him back to the front door. The detective had matters in hand. Sidney Dalton would be apprehended on sight. There was absolutely no reason for me to get involved. Except I needed to see things to their conclusion, or the itch at the base of my brain would never leave me alone.

The next day, I jumped off the tram and joined the flow of people heading along the road. I hurried the best I could to the spot where the grand performance was being held on the foreshore. Petone Beach bustled with excitement as Wellingtonians gathered for the re-enactment of Captain Cook's historic landing. A platform in the prime position was set up for the royal visitor and the dignitaries. I sat at the edge of the crowd on the grass and scanned the sea of faces for any sign of either Detective Archer or Lieutenant Dalton. My heart raced with anticipation; time was running out, and we needed to stop the lieutenant before he could carry out his sinister plan.

A roar went up as the sun glinted off the gleaming white hull of the prince's launch as it cut through the waves, approaching the shore with grace and precision. The crowd erupted into cheers and applause, their excitement palpable. I rose to my tiptoes, craning my neck to catch a glimpse of the heir to the throne, while scanning the throng for any sign of the detective.

"Long live Prince Edward!" someone shouted, and the crowd took up the cry, their voices blending into a cacophony of adoration.

As the prince disembarked from his launch, stepping onto the sand with practised poise, I couldn't help but feel a pang of sympathy for him. He appeared tired, the strain of his never-ending royal duties evident in the lines etched across his face. And yet he smiled and waved, every inch of him the perfect heir apparent.

Once seated, the noise died down as everyone waited for the play to begin. The ocean breeze tousled my hair, the scent of salt and seaweed filling my nostrils. From a vessel anchored not far from shore, a dinghy was launched filled with eager actors in period costume. The sailors rowed towards the shore. At the bow, a man dressed as Captain Cook wavered unsteadily, then he toppled forward and gripped the edge of the dinghy for dear life.

"Look at him! Captain Cook doesn't seem to have his sea legs today," a woman beside me remarked with a giggle.

"Perhaps it is just nerves," I murmured, my thoughts still consumed by my search for Detective Archer and Lieutenant Dalton. Amidst the laughter and merriment, my heart raced, a constant reminder of the danger lurking beneath the surface of this seemingly innocent event. I wondered if we would find Lieutenant Dalton in time. Or if we were already too late.

As the dinghy approached the shoreline, a wave swept under it, causing the vessel to lurch. Captain Cook, unable to maintain his precarious balance, tumbled into the water. The crowd roared with laughter, clapping and cheering at the unexpected spectacle. The actor playing the lead floundered in the surf, struggling to regain his footing as he staggered towards the sand. The gathered Māori actors, wearing traditional garb and with moko painted on their faces, confronted him with mock aggression, mingled with amusement and irritation. It became painfully obvious that the man portraying the legendary explorer was inebriated, his speech slurred and movements clumsy.

"Goodness, he must've drowned his nerves in spirits, and now he's making a fool of himself in front of everyone," I muttered. Poor fellow, his acting career would be ruined over this.

Drawing my attention away from the play, I focused on my main purpose. What had the lieutenant planned in memory of his father? The thought of all these innocent people caught in the crossfire of Lieutenant Dalton's vendetta against the prince filled me with dread. And yet, deep down, I couldn't help but feel sympathy for the lieutenant. His desire for justice, albeit seriously misguided, stemmed from a place of love for his father.

Crossfire. No. A rifle didn't fit into what snippets I had gathered. My conversation with Miss Belmont flitted through my mind. How Mr Novikoff had given Mr Dalton a broken radio that he was obsessed with. The items from Adam Dalton's satchel that scattered when he was killed. Wire and pliers. We assumed he had been some electrical worker. But what if the Dalton brothers and Mr Novikoff were making a bomb? I had no idea how one actually made a bomb. The limit of my knowledge was that it involved wires, dynamite and some sort of...timepiece.

"Oh," I breathed out and jumped to my feet.

The laughter and cheers of the crowd grew louder as the re-enactment continued, filling the air with an eerie juxtaposition of joy and impending doom. I had to find Detective Archer. Pushing through the throng of spectators, I scanned the sea of faces for any sign of the detective. Finally, I spotted a familiar broad figure in a well-cut suit standing at the outer edge of the crowd closest to the prince. Even from a distance, I could see the worry lines etched in his face. Without having to ask, I knew that he'd had no luck finding his quarry.

"Detective Archer!" I called out his name and hoped he heard me above the laughter.

He turned, and a flash of warmth passed behind his eyes before it was replaced with annoyance as I joined him. "Mrs Devine. I told you to stay away. It's not safe."

"It is just as well I did come out. I have remembered something Miss Belmont said to me. That the lieutenant is obsessed with an old radio. That made me think of when Mr Dalton was hit by the tram and the contents of his satchel scattered on the road. It held bits of wire and pliers. I thought he might have done electrical work, but what if the brothers were up to something else?"

"A bomb," the detective murmured in a low tone so no one else overheard. "If he used something for a timer, he doesn't even have to be here."

"Like a pocket watch that belonged to his father?" I suggested.

"I'm not sure how reliable one with a bullet hole in it would be. We need to find it. I'll alert the lads to hunt out any radios among the props." Detective Archer ground his jaw as he glanced at me. Perhaps considering if he should order me away.

"If I find either the lieutenant or the radio, I'll... scream." I cut off any attempt to shoo me away. Screaming struck me as the best way to attract attention over the din from both the performance and the audience.

He nodded, but a quick smile flashed across his face. He moved to spread the word among his men. Meanwhile, the play continued its disastrous course. Captain Cook careened across the makeshift stage like a ship adrift in a storm, stumbling over props and causing chaos among the actors. His antics drew a mixture of laughter and concern from the audience, but the prince seemed less than amused, judging by the terse expression on his face.

"Blimey!" someone cried out, eliciting laughter from the audience as the drunken actor stumbled into a penned-off area where the Māori kept their pigs. With a loud crash, he collided with the enclosure, sending splintered wood flying and releasing one of the ornery swine.

The pig, now free from its pen, charged headlong into the crowd and caused people to scream with a mix of delight and terror. The creature trampled over children unceremoniously, leaving them sprawled on the ground in its wake. Then the pig veered off course and lunged for a fallen woman's hat. It snatched the delicate creation from her head with surprising dexterity, causing her to let out a high-pitched scream. The pig then proceeded to munch contentedly on the vibrant flowers adorning her once-pristine bonnet.

I couldn't help but chuckle, despite the gravity of my mission. The sight was undeniably comical. I glanced over at Prince Edward, who sat stone-faced in his seat, no doubt wondering why he had bothered to grace Petone with his royal presence. The heir to the

British throne was not amused. He sat stiffly in his chair, clearly struggling to maintain his composure as the disastrous re-enactment floundered on.

The Mayor of Petone, a portly gentleman with beads of sweat forming on his forehead, was mortified beyond belief. "Someone get that blasted actor off the stage!" he bellowed, trying to regain some semblance of control.

"Stay focused, Grace," I reminded myself as absurdity unfolded around me. The first tendrils of panic coiled in my stomach. We were running out of time, and the situation was becoming more chaotic by the second.

In the midst of the uproar and confusion, I finally spotted his figure emerging from behind a painted scene of heavily forested hills. Lieutenant Dalton.

"Detective Archer!" I yelled as loud as I could.

Fortunately, we had not strayed too far apart, and he heard me. The policeman's gaze followed my outstretched finger, and his eyes widened in recognition. We wove our way through the panicked and disoriented spectators, our every step fuelled by a burning sense of urgency as we converged on the conspirator.

"I'll deal to him," he said to me as he forged off after the lieutenant.

With my slender build, I couldn't tackle a soldier, so I left the detective and his policemen to arrest the conspirator. But I could confront a small household appliance.

"Where is it?" I muttered under my breath, pushing through the throngs of people to get closer to the stage. The uproar had only grown louder, drowning out my frantic thoughts and making it near-impossible to concentrate. I scanned the area around the painted scenery for any clue that might lead me to the radio. And then, like a bolt of lightning, it hit me. If I were an anarchist hell-bent on blowing up the prince, where would I hide my deadly weapon?

As close as possible, while still being able to pass unnoticed. My attention turned to what lay between the prince and the stage. A table set up with refreshments. The rogue pig from earlier resurfaced, bursting from between legs and careening into the table in an attempt to grab a spot of afternoon tea. The porker's weight was sufficient to knock the laden table over. As the crowd shrieked and the pig feasted, my gaze fell upon the object revealed when the tablecloth was snatched away. The radio!

With adrenaline coursing through my veins, I dashed towards it and snatched it up. Spinning, I elbowed people out of my way and ran towards the beach. The sand beneath my feet shifted and slid, but determination kept me moving towards the water's edge. The dinghy bobbed in the shallows and gave me an idea.

I placed the radio on the seat. Then, with a heave, I shoved the small boat out into the receding tide, watching its progress with bated breath. The little boat drifted further out to sea. Keeping my eye on it, I hoped that I was wrong and there was no bomb, but if there was, that I had grabbed the right thing.

I risked a glance behind me, and the weight of the world seemed to lift from my shoulders, as Detective Archer subdued Lieutenant Dalton and snapped handcuffs around his wrists.

Meanwhile, the action of the ocean pulled the dinghy further and further out into the harbour.

"Please, let it be far enough," I whispered.

The explosion caught us all off guard. The loud *whump* made me throw up my arms. The dinghy disappeared in a plume of smoke and water. Debris flew high into the sky, only to rain back down on the ocean. Thankfully, it had detonated far enough away that the blast caused no damage.

On the foreshore, people screamed and cried out, not sure if the plumes of smoke were part of the play. Many surged back up the beach to put more distance between them and the disintegrated boat. The policemen formed a tight knot of protection around the prince.

"Bravo! What a magnificent end to the performance!" Prince Edward called out, and he rose to his feet to clap.

Everyone cheered and joined in, thinking it was all part of the planned festivities.

As I walked back up the sand, to my surprise, the gathered onlookers began to applaud. Their faces alight with bemusement and relief. They laughed and cheered, mistakenly convinced that the entire spectacle had been purely for their entertainment.

"Bravo!" one woman shouted, clapping her hands together with gusto.

"Realistic, wasn't it?" another chimed in, nudging his companion with a knowing wink.

"Who would have thought the Māori would bomb Captain Cook's boat?" a third added, laughter bubbling up in their voice.

Skirting around the assembled people, I made my way to where the detective and his policemen stood. Lieutenant Dalton was loaded into the back of an idling motor vehicle.

I exchanged a glance with the detective, and we both stifled relieved chuckles at the absurdity of the situation. It seemed our efforts to protect the innocent had been mistaken for mere theatrics.

"All's well that ends well," Detective Archer said and winked.

Chapter Twenty

As I stood there, my shoes and the hem of my dress soaked through with seawater, I couldn't help but grin. The prince was safe, the would-be assassin had been apprehended, and everyone was none the wiser as to the true drama that had unfolded before their eyes.

"I think I will stick to my sewing. This is all far too much excitement for my heart." And my wardrobe. My shoes were probably ruined, but I would try to sponge the salt water from the leather.

"I will have one of the lads drive you home, Mrs Devine. It is the least we can do, to thank you for your help." Detective Archer touched the brim of his fedora and called a uniformed officer over.

Later that afternoon, I was having a well-deserved rest on the sofa when a rap came at the front door. Grumbling under my breath, I dropped my stocking-clad feet to the ground and answered the door. A man in a chauffeur's livery stood on my doorstep, but there was no motor vehicle in sight. He had most probably parked as close as he dared on the narrow and twisty road.

"Mrs Devine?" There was a clipped British edge to his words.

"Yes." He was most likely the driver for a client who needed an urgent repair before tonight's ball. We didn't have a telephone in our house, so a note would be the only way to reach me when I wasn't at the atelier.

He handed me a thick cream envelope and then walked away. I stared at it as I shut the door and returned to my spot on the sofa. Lifting the flap with my thumbnail, I pulled out the sheet of paper.

"Who was that?" Dad called out from the kitchen.

I read the words on the note twice, before pulling out the card tucked inside the envelope. "My fairy godmother. Apparently, Cinderella is going to the ball."

My involvement in saving the royal personage would never be made public. Besides, who would believe a story about a drunken Captain Cook and a pig running amok? But my actions would not go unrewarded. The prince had extended an invitation to the Citizens Ball. I doubt it really came from the heir to the throne. This had the feel of Mrs Cooper pulling strings. Or cornering diplomats until she got exactly what she wanted.

"The ball? What will you wear?" Dad had hopped to the opening that separated the lounge and kitchen.

"I have a little something that might just do." I grinned, then excitement bloomed through me, and I flung myself at Dad and hugged him. "I have to go! Lots to do!"

With the help of Sam and Etty, I was scrubbed, my hair styled, and my dress was absolutely perfect. Lacking a pumpkin to turn into a coach, instead, I walked the short distance from my premises to the Town Hall. Once I showed the invitation, I was allowed inside, where I joined the queue with dozens of excited people. Luckily, I had a gown to wear that ensured I didn't feel like the pauper about to meet the prince. I had donned my fairytale fantail dress, and the feathered train swished behind me.

The line edged forwards, and soon it was my turn. I curtseyed, as Mrs Cooper had taught me.

Prince Edward took my hand. "Lovely to meet you," he said in a bored tone.

As our hands slid apart, his thumb grazed the top of my glove. For a mere second, his bare skin brushed across the back of my hand, and I cast my eyes downwards as the memory thrust into my mind.

A pen scratched over paper as he wrote a desperate letter home. '...I loathe every moment parted from you. Here I am surrounded by dour ham-faced women. I cannot wait to have you in my arms again...'

That would be a blow to all the hopeful women present. It seemed the prince had already given his heart to another. In that brief moment that I glimpsed what went on in his head, I suspected that for all that he played the dutiful son, Prince Edward would give up the throne for the woman he loved.

Determined to enjoy myself, I collected a glass of champagne and stood at the edges of the dance floor, humming along to the music and tapping my toes. This was a world I was never meant to inhabit. With the meet and greet over, the prince kicked off the dancing by claiming Miss Belmont. Her gown shimmering with all the diamantés sewn into the pink chiffon. I huffed at his private words. How dare he call my most stunning client ham-faced!

Miss Novikoff prowled the edge of the dance floor. When hopeful men approached her, she spat harsh words at them that saw them hurriedly retreat. I wondered why she didn't dance when she could have had her pick of the elite of Wellington. Certainly, they circled and vied for their chance.

Then I saw the way she watched Miss Belmont, and I had an inkling of an idea why she didn't want to dance with Prince Edward or any other man.

Her prowling brought her close to me, and I thought I would try again to break through her tough exterior. "Miss Belmont looks lovely this evening. I am glad she decided to come after what happened to the lieutenant."

"I convinced her to accompany me. That man did not deserve her, and now he has broken her heart. Men. Why do women bother?" She turned her dark eyes to me with that last question.

There were some days that I agreed with her. But men weren't all bad. Some were kind and honourable. I took another sip of champagne. While nervous to be among such refined company, I relaxed a little from the combination of music and wine. Seizing a moment of bravery, I spoke quietly and without looking directly at Miss Novikoff. "Some women don't bother with them. I have a friend who, if she had been here, would ignore every man, including the prince, and would only want to dance with Miss Belmont. Or you." Both women were beautiful but in two very different ways.

"You would call such a person your friend?" she scoffed, but curiosity lit her eyes.

"Of course. She is my best friend in the entire world. Who she prefers as a dance partner makes no difference to me. I love her dearly because of the way she is made." The Russian woman might have monetary riches, but she didn't have a friendship like that between me and Sam. Miss Belmont might become such a friend and ally for her. If she knew the truth. There was the risk she held the same narrow prejudices as many others, but I doubted it given her open and warm personality.

Miss Novikoff stared at me and, for the first time in our acquaintance, the angry look dropped from her face and pain washed over her features.

"It is difficult...to find such dance partners in a cruel world," she whispered, as though she had never dared voice the concern to anyone else before.

A pang of sadness rang through me for the other woman. Perhaps her haughty attitude was to cover her loneliness. "Yes. It is not an easy path to walk. But there are those who understand, and there are places that are open-minded about different combinations on the dance floor."

"How would a person find such a place?" She licked her lips and glanced around to ensure we weren't overheard.

"I could ask my friend to introduce an interested person to such clubs and others they could trust. Perhaps during a fitting?" I lowered my tone as the dance ended and Miss Belmont rushed over to us.

"Yes. Thank you, Mrs Devine." She smiled, a genuine thing that lit her face and filled her gaze with hope.

For a brief moment, I wondered if Miss Novikoff and Sam would get along. I did joke about finding a wealthy girlfriend for her. But then the two of them might be too opinionated and stubborn. I could imagine their arguments echoing off the hills around Wellington if they disagreed. Perhaps it would be better not to suggest that, but Sam could ease Miss Novikoff into some more welcoming circles.

Miss Belmont linked arms with her friend. "I say Mrs D, you're looking fab! That bird gown suits you to a T."

A slow blush heated my skin at being treated like an equal by the wealthy women. "Thank you, Miss

Belmont. You are lovely enough to entice the prince to stay in New Zealand."

The young socialite scoffed. "A bit quiet for my liking. Come on, Leena. I promised Mrs D we'd get photographed."

"You should dance with somebody, Leena," an older voice called out.

Mrs Novikoff joined us, wearing a deep green gown that pooled over her shoes. I wish she'd let me hem it up a good six inches.

"And so she shall, Mrs Novikoff." Miss Belmont giggled and pulled her friend out onto the dance floor.

"That is not what I meant," the older Russian woman muttered.

"They are enjoying the evening and there is no harm in it. Even if the Town Hall is not as grand as the palaces of the tsar." I don't know what made me do it, but as I mentioned their far-off homeland, I rested my hand on Mrs Novikoff's arm, at her elbow where her glove stopped. I had tugged off one glove earlier to fuss with the feathers on my gown.

The memory danced into my brain in time with the music. I stood at the edge of a glittering ballroom such as I had never seen before.

Leena, young, innocent, in a dress of midnight blue encrusted in beads, walked across the floor. Pride swelled in my chest. My only daughter was a beautiful creature who would surely catch the eye of the young prince.

'She is destined for great things,' a deep voice murmured from beside me.

I turned to face the monk, and a chill raced down my spine. 'Yes. I see a match between her and Alexei, despite the difference in their ages.'

He grinned and his black eyes glinted like obsidian. With one bejewelled hand, he stroked his beard. 'That is one possibility. But he is a boy. No. I see a far greater future for her. I shall have her and make her my consort.'

No! The denial screamed through me.

'Do not think about denying me, Madame Novikoff. Wherever you go, I shall call her to me.' The monk held out one hand and murmured something under his breath.

As though she were a wind-up toy, Leena stopped mid-step, pivoted on her heel, and then headed directly to him. She placed her hand on his outstretched one and smiled up at him.

Fear for my daughter cascaded through me. Wherever you go...well, we shall see about that. There would be somewhere in this world beyond his mystical reach, where my daughter would be safe.

"Rasputin," I murmured without realising it.

Mrs Novikoff widened her eyes and glanced at her daughter, taking the lead as she danced with Miss Belmont. "He cannot reach her here," she hissed.

"No. He is dead." I had read the stories of the man who had once stood close to the tsar and tsarina, and who gathered many enemies. Rasputin had been poisoned, shot, strangled, and thrown into a freezing river.

"Death would not stop him. But several oceans have. Spirits cannot cross that much water." The wild look in her eyes settled. Perhaps she remembered her surroundings.

Now I understood why a mother would move her family such a vast distance—to ensure her daughter was safe from a predator's grasp.

Her eyes narrowed, and she blew out a snort. Probably remembering that I was the hired help, and she shouldn't be talking to me. Then she hurried away.

"Mrs Devine?" a quiet voice said from beside me.

I turned to find Detective Archer, and my mind hiccupped. Gosh, he was handsome in evening wear. His dark hair was glossy and slicked back like rain on a piece of obsidian. The width of his shoulders was expertly displayed in the tailcoat.

He bowed before me and held out one hand. "Might I have the pleasure of this dance?"

It took me only a second to decide that yes, he could. Then I took a few longer seconds to plead with my gift. *Please don't show me anything while we dance.* I wanted to enjoy the moment, not see him shaving earlier that evening, or trying to understand what the old woman was saying, or worse—have some hideous flashback to the war. To make sure, I smoothed my glove back over my fingers.

Worry flickered behind his eyes at my delayed response. "If you are waiting for someone else..." He glanced over his shoulder to where Prince Edward took the hand of another bright young socialite who fancied herself the next Princess of Wales.

"No, gosh, I thought you might prefer to dance with someone else." I hadn't planned to dance with anyone, not wanting to embarrass myself by saying the wrong thing.

"No. I sought you out because I would like to dance with you." He curled the fingers of his offered hand.

The intensity of his gaze heated me as much as if I stood with my bottom to a roaring fire. I smiled and placed my hand on his. "Yes, you may have this dance, Detective Archer."

"Benjamin," he murmured as he took my hand and we walked onto the dance floor.

"Excuse me?" I turned to face him. Our joined hands raised, and my other on his shoulder as he lightly placed his at my waist.

"My name is Benjamin. I think given the events of the last week, you should call me by my Christian name." The band played a fast tune, and the detective swirled me around before we fell into step with the others around us.

"Benjamin." I rolled his name across my tongue. It suited him, being a solid, dependable name. "And I insist that you call me Grace." I had no ownership over the title of Mrs Devine and much preferred my first name, or my family surname of Sullivan, if I was able to choose.

"Your dress is lovely, Grace," he said as we moved

seamlessly together. Unsurprisingly, he was a natural leader on the dance floor. He led without being forceful, creating a space that invited you to move towards him.

"Thank you. My inspiration was a...a *piwakawaka*." I nearly stumbled over the word but thought I had the pronunciation correct.

His eyebrows arched, then he murmured. "*Ka pai*. Not many people know the Māori word for the fantail. But you have chosen an odd bird to inspire you. Some consider them messengers who bring news of death."

I glanced down at the bronze feathers edging my bodice. When I dreamed up the design, I didn't realise I was creating a gown to represent a deathly messenger. "I didn't know that. I have always found comfort in their presence. There is one that often accompanies me through the Botanic Garden, and he always seems to have much to say."

Benjamin pulled me closer, and I inhaled his clean and slightly lemony scent.

"My grandmother, my *tupuna wahine*, has a different view. She always told me that the *piwakawka* appears to warn you to be prepared for change."

I liked that interpretation better than them being omens of death. "I've seen much change in my life. Perhaps my little friends were right."

As we danced, I was certain about one thing. First thing when I saw her, I could inform Etty that she was correct. Detective Archer, or Benjamin, was a most excellent dancer.

It might only be a town hall in Wellington at the bottom of the world, but I was wearing my dream gown and danced with a kind and honourable man. This was my Cinderella moment. Let the other women circle the prince. I found joy in the moments, and people, they overlooked.

THE END

Historical notes

Anzac Biscuits

The Anzac biscuit is a sweet biscuit, popular in Australia and New Zealand. These treats were sent by wives and women's groups to soldiers abroad. These treats would often have to endure a lengthy journey (sometimes lasting several months due to naval transportation) and it was important to use a recipe with ingredients that would not spoil easily. Traditional Anzac biscuits were comprised of rolled oats, sugar, plain flour, coconut, butter, golden syrup or treacle, bicarbonate of soda and boiling water. A recipe without eggs made the perfect candidate for the task. Anzac biscuits have long been associated with the Australian and New Zealand Army Corps established in World War I. The first ones are believed to have been made in 1916, but an official recipe didn't appear until 1921 in the *St Andrew's Cookery Book*.

Ingredients:

1 cup rolled oats

1 cup flour

1 cup coconut threads

1 cup soft brown sugar

¼ cup golden syrup

125 g butter

2 Tbsp boiling water

½ tsp baking soda

Method:

Preheat oven to 160°C fan bake and line 2 oven trays with baking paper for easy clean-up.

Combine rolled oats, flour, coconut and sugar in a large bowl.

Heat together golden syrup, butter and boiling water until butter melts.

Stir in baking soda, then mix into dry ingredients until well combined.

Roll mixture into balls slightly smaller than a golf ball and place on trays, allowing a little room for spreading.

For biscuits that are crunchy on the outside but a little chewy inside, lightly flatten with a fork or damp fingers and bake for 20–25 minutes. For chunky, super-hard biscuits, bake for 30–35 minutes. For very crunchy thin biscuits, press dough very flat and bake for 15 minutes.

Allow to cool on the trays (they will harden on cooling) before transferring to an airtight container. They will keep fresh for several weeks.

The Māori Battalion

There were mixed views among Māori about the Great War. Some rushed to sign up. Others opposed the war or didn't want to fight for England due to the damage done to their communities in the previous century.

The Empire had an imperial policy that was opposed to native people fighting alongside Europeans and they were indeed concerned about an uprising or Māori soldiers expecting equal treatment! In the Great War, the Māori Pioneer Battalion, or Native Contingent and Pioneer Battalion, included Pacific Islanders as well as Māori, and Māori also enlisted in other battalions. But in 1940 a unit reserved for Māori was raised at their request, the 28th (Māori) Battalion, to serve with the New Zealand Army. It became widely known as just 'Māori Battalion'. In this book I have chosen to use this common name, rather than the one in use in 1920. Some 2,000 Māori fought alongside their Pākehā (white) comrades in the Great War. Some say that it was only in battle that many New Zealanders saw Māori as individuals for the first time. Ironic that our lads had to go as far as Gallipoli and France to find out about themselves and each other.

The Royal Visit

Edward, Prince of Wales (who later reigned briefly as Edward VIII), visited New Zealand in 1920 as part of a month-long tour to thank the country for its contribution to the Great War. The visit was indeed marred by a series of unfortunate events in Wellington.

A young boy was run over by his motorcade, both the boy's legs being crushed. Despite his injury, the lad remained in good spirits and still waved his flag as he was carried off.

The temporary grandstand at Newtown Park did indeed collapse. Although the day before the prince arrived to inspect the troops, not just before his arrival, as I have it.

And...as fanciful and made up as it sounds (or in a case of authors can't make this stuff up!) the re-enactment of Captain Cook's landing did indeed have a drunk actor and a rampaging pig.

At night, the prince grimaced his way through banquets and balls, as he wrote to his lover at the time, Freda Dudley Ward. "We stuck it out like heroes till the supper and tried to lug those wads of ham-faced women around, although we were all feeling very weary and thoroughly peeved."

In 1936, King Edward VIII would abdicate his throne for the woman he loved—American divorcee Mrs Wallis Simpson.

Also by Tilly Wallace

For the most complete and up to date list of books, please visit the website:

https://tillywallace.com/books/

Available series:

Tournament of Shadows

Manner and Monsters

Highland Wolves

Grace Designs Mysteries

About the Author

Tilly drinks entirely too much coffee and is obsessed with hats. When not scouring vintage stores for her next chapeau purchase, she writes whimsical historical fantasy novels, set in a bygone time where magic is real. With a quirky and loveable cast, her books combine vintage magic and gentle humour.

If you love found family and comfort reads, then come and escape reality with me.

Email: tilly@tillywallace.com
Web: https://www.tillywallace.com
STORE: https://www.tillywallacebooks.com

facebook.com/tillywallaceauthor

bookbub.com/authors/tilly-wallace

goodreads.com/tillywallace

instagram.com/tillywallaceauthor

www.ingramcontent.com/pod-product-compliance
Lightning Source LLC
Chambersburg PA
CBHW061815190726
48289CB00007B/2205